We were surrounded by enemies. There was only one way out.

Speak them not but hold them in your memory, Mlada the witch-woman had said as she wrote the words in the ground in the letters of the common tongue. *When you are in dire need, give tongue to them and your enemies will flee.*

If this wasn't a time of dire need, then I would never be in dire need.

I stepped to the front and faced my enemies. Just as the host of beast men began to lumber toward us, clubs upraised, I lifted my hands and at the top of my great bass voice I thundered out the three words that Mlada had taught me.

The terrified creatures threw their clubs away—and fled.

THE
ALIEN

by

Victor Besaw

FAWCETT GOLD MEDAL • NEW YORK

THE ALIEN

© 1979 Victor Besaw

Published by Fawcett Gold Medal Books, a unit of CBS Publications, the Consumer Publishing Division of CBS Inc.

ISBN: 0-449-14197-7

Printed in the United States of America

10 9 8 7 6 5 4 3 2 1

All that I could see from where I stood
was a tiny stone-built cottage and a wood
of giant, darkling trees. A sullen stream
erupted like a sluggish, silent scream
from out the grasping tunnel of the trees.
A place accursed of all divinities . . .
a demon-haunted fastness, on whose sod
the wandering foot of man had never trod.
Fear, like a god, rode on the very air . . .
stouthearted must he be who travels there.
                              —*The Song of Godranec*

Prologue

Outside Gelsan on the road to Malkha Voet,
on the third day of the year of Lilkhanflet*
Bdengi got himself a strange new thrall . . .
a small Nyarlethu, scarce five mangi† tall.
                    —*The Song of Godranec*

The Vilarian double sun was almost touching the horizon, and the broad road with its green fringe of nythan trees stretched as straight as Chalkhrondu engineers could make it. An ornate carriage drawn by two tailless delkhator lizards was rattling swiftly homeward toward Gelsan, which loomed in the near distance. The cool of evening was beginning to spread through the land after the scorching heat of the day. Inside the carriage Bdengi and his wife were enjoying the cool breeze, which blew in from the forbidden wierwoods across the Volsek River to the west.

* *Lilkhanflet:* The year of the flying fire-lizard in the old tongue.
† *mangi:* Four inches, Earth.

Bdengi was pleased with himself. Life was good if you had money and power, and in Chalkhrondu, even a blacksmith could rise to importance, especially if he happened to be astute enough to marry a woman who had money. Bdengi was light of skin and bald of head, with a well-tended, luxuriant black beard. His eyes were brown, small, and close together, and the layers of fat on him couldn't hide the powerful muscles which were a heritage of his years as a blacksmith.

Bdengi was never far from a winecup, even on a trip. He had in his hand a bejeweled golden cup full of the purple juice of the grape which he loved, and was about to sip from it. Of a sudden the carriage stopped abruptly, spilling the purple fluid on the white silken doublet that covered Bdengi's ample stomach.

"Haldor!" he roared. "Haldor!"

A door slid aside in the front of the carriage and a frightened, wrinkled old face appeared in the opening.

"Yes, vlan?" said Haldor in a timid voice.

"May Khanophet and all the demons of the underworld grind your miserable living bones to powder, you wretch! What do you mean by stopping so abruptly? Look what you've done to my doublet? I'll have your head for this!"

"I'm sorry, vlan, but the delkhators stopped of themselves before I could prevent. Look what's in the road up ahead."

Bdengi stood up and, opening a panel in the roof, stuck his head out and looked. The delkhators were shuffling nervously in their harness and snorting. About a hundred paces in front of the carriage a strange little creature was toddling down the middle of the road, naked save for a breechclout, and weeping in an odd, high-pitched voice.

Verla, Bdengi's wife, thrust her head out of the panel beside her husband's and looked.

"What is it, Zhen?" she asked.

"It looks like a Nyarlethu baby up ahead."

"What's a dwarf doing this far south—and a baby at that?"

"I saw a huge bird rise from here a while ago, vlana," said Haldor. "It looked like a skaldu. I wondered what it was doing so far south."

Bdengi was as benevolent as any of his race ever gets . . . which isn't saying a great deal. He shrugged and turned to the guard on the jump seat on the rear of the carriage.

"Kill it, Arlo. We can't sit here all night."

The guard raised his bow, when Verla laid her hand on Bdengi's arm. "No, Zhen; don't kill it."

Bdengi frowned. "Why not?"

"I think it's cute. I want it; get it for me."

Bdengi shrugged. "All right. Arlo . . . go and catch the thing so we can get home. I want a bath."

After a short chase, Arlo caught the little creature and dumped it inside the carriage, which was soon under way again.

THE ALIEN

The baby was a chubby, healthy Nyarlethu child with curly brown hair on its head. It had pointed, slightly furry ears. Just in front of his ears two tiny nubbin horns sprouted. Nothing like it had ever been seen in Gelsan before. The Chalkhrondu stared at it in wonder, and it stared back solemnly with its large, slanted, slit-pupiled eyes.

"I wonder if it can talk?" Verla asked.

"I can talk," piped the child.

"What's your name, child?" asked Verla.

"Godranec."

"Where are you from?"

Godranec waved a tiny arm toward the north. "Up there . . . from mountains . . . far away."

"How'd you get down here?" asked Bdengi.

"Big bird carried me here."

"Where are your people?"

"Can't say it in your tongue. I'm hungry."

Verla fished around in the picnic hamper at her feet and extracted a piece of roasted tharg* flesh and handed it to the dwarf.

Godranec seized it and tore into it with his tiny sharp teeth. "Good . . ." he said between bites. "Thank you."

So Godranec, the alien, found a new home, and Bdengi found a new thrall. The dwarf was not to leave Gelsan for many a long year.

---

* *tharg*: A horned quadruped somewhat larger than a goat which is abundant all over the planet. Much prized for its flesh. It is found wild as well as domesticated.

1

The food Bdengi ate within his halls
was flavored by the blood of helpless thralls,
for Kula's whip caused pain and anguish sore—
and some were beat to earth to rise no more.
　　　　　　　　—The Song of Godranec

My early childhood was spent in luxury. I seldom
left my vlana's* private quarters, where I was show-
ered with all sorts of rich food and attention. I was
a sort of pet, not only to the vlana but also to the
other ladies there. I was clothed in rich robes and
was very happy. I knew I was different from those
around me, but, pampered and petted by the vlana
and her maids, it never dawned on me how utterly
alien I was. Then gradually her attitude toward me
changed as I grew older, and I was no longer
happy.

She grew cold and distant, for, with the years,
my horns grew until they were as long as the

* *vlana*: Chalkhrondu for "mistress."

vlana's middle finger. My body also lost its smoothness and grew more hairy. Not furry, like a beast; but I had far more body hair than the Chalkhrondi had.

I still had a need to be loved and wanted, and the vlana had been a sort of surrogate mother to me. Though . . . there was a picture in the back of my mind of a flowery vale and another face, much like my own, beaming at me with gentleness and love . . . then came the shadow of a great bird flying through the air. I knew not what these fantasies meant, but they refused to go away, and the vale, the face, and the mountains were ever in my mind.

The vlana kept growing more and more cold and abrupt to me. Finally, unable to endure it longer, I knelt before her and embraced her knees.

"What have I done, vlana?" I pleaded. "Why are you so angry and cold with me?"

To my surprise she spurned me with her foot, sending me halfway across the room.

"Don't ever touch me again," she snapped. "Stay away from me."

"But why, vlana?"

"No matter why . . . just keep away from me."

Just then the Vlan Bdengi came in. Noting the tension in the room, with me over in the corner trying my best not to cry and the vlana sitting at her dressing table with her face like a thundercloud, he said, "What's the matter here?" He smiled indulgently, which, on him, looked like a grimace.

"The trouble is that I can't stand that little monster a moment longer," she snapped.

Vlan Bdengi raised his eyebrows, "I thought you said he was cute."

"He was . . . when he was little. Now he's as hairy as a tharg, and his ugliness repels me. Take him away."

"What'll I do with him?"

"I don't care what you do with your thralls. Kill him, beat him, free him . . . do anything, but get him out of here," she almost screamed.

Bdengi shrugged. "All right. Come along, Godranec."

I followed him quietly, my jaw set stubbornly. I was determined not to show emotion before these people if it killed me.

I was taken to a garden in the back of the house where a door was opened and I found myself in a small room, not a bad room as rooms go. It was sparsely furnished, with a washstand and pitcher, a table, several pegs on the walls for clothing (which I didn't have), and a narrow bed against one wall. There was an oil lamp on the table, with flint and steel to light it with, and a ceramic jug in the corner, no doubt containing oil for the lamp.

"This will be your room, Godranec," said Bdengi. "I'll see that someone brings you heavier clothing and a cloak to keep you warm. It's late in the day now, so get something to eat, and rest. You're seven years old now and strong, so I ought to get a little use out of you. Tomorrow morning I'll take you to the kitchens."

I made the sign of obedience. "Yes, vlan."

When he had gone I threw myself down on the bed and wept bitterly. When my storm of passion had died, I got up and went to the large, cracked mirror fastened to one wall and looked critically at myself.

My only standard of beauty was that of the humans among which I had been raised. In the mirror I saw a thing not quite half the size of a human but built thick and blocky. My face was square and bony and my eyes were slanted and slit-pupiled and there was trouble in their brown depths. Worst of all were the pointed, furry ears and the two horns of a handspan long that sprouted from my forehead. Even in my own eyes I was misshapen and ugly. No wonder the vlana had rejected me. I was most definitely not human. What was I then? Where had I come from? Still I had the memory of the flowery vale in the mountains and a soft woman-face of my own people. Was it a dream? I didn't know. Nobody had ever told me where I had come from, and I thirsted to know. I was most definitely not from Gelsan. Where could I find others of my race? Somewhere in the mountains of the north, was all I knew . . . but that covered a lot of territory. Questions, questions, questions . . . with no answers.

My troubled thoughts were interrupted when a

little serving maid appeared with an armful of clothing for me. The thin silken robe I had worn in the vlana's quarters was inadequate here, and I was cold. The maid put the clothing on the bed and left hurriedly without speaking.

There were two or three pairs of breeches of warm tharg-wool, a doublet of flexible leather, and a warm woolen cloak against the chill. All were worn but serviceable. I put on a pair of the woolen socks that came with the breeches, put on a pair of the breeches, bound on the sandals, and hung the rest of the clothing on the pegs on the wall. Then I put on my doublet and my cloak and went to supper.

I had never been in the thralls' dining room but I knew where it was. It was a large, plain room with long plain tables, and plain wooden benches to sit on. It smelled of greasy stew and stale bread. I got a metal tray from a stack and got into line. The thralls in line with me, as well as those who were serving, looked at me oddly but said nothing for good or evil. Without a word being said, they made it plain that they wished to have nothing to do with me. This added to my hurt, but I was determined not to let them see how much it mattered. I got my food and went to a far corner away from everybody else and ate. Probably because of my hunger, I found the stew to be much better to the taste than it was to the eye. I even discovered that the stale bread was delicious when soaked in the gravy.

After a restless night, I came back from a breakfast of bread, cheese, and vlas, a sort of tea made from the aromatic leaves of a bush that grows profusely all over the continent, to find Bdengi waiting for me. He greeted me pleasantly enough and conducted me to the kitchen.

The kitchen was an immense room, somewhat separated from the rest of the palace, and it had several huge fireplaces. A couple of the fireplaces were in a sort of pit with a hood above them to lead the smoke out through the ceiling. They were rigged up with a spit so whole animals could be roasted at a time. There were many tables for preparing food and a large metal sink where dishes could be washed. The kitchen was filled with the odor of roasting tharg, of baking bread, and a multitude of other odors, some of which I couldn't identify.

The cook in charge was a huge, burly personage with a beefy, mottled face that showed a love of wine. The age and sex of the creature were indeterminate, but since it was dressed as a woman, I accepted her as such.

She waddled up and bowed to Bdengi (something that gave her problems, due to a tendency to fall forward on her face).

"Could you use another thrall out here, Kula?" Bdengi asked.

"Yes, lord . . . even such an one as that." Her voice was rough and deep, much like a man's.

"Very well. You'll serve here, Godranec, until I put you somewhere else."

I made the sign of obedience. "Yes, vlan."

He left abruptly and Kula snarled at me, "Come with me, you little beast."

I followed her to one of the pits, where a whole tharg was being roasted. A crank thrust out from one side, and a thin little girl not much taller than I was struggling valiantly with it but finding it almost too much for her.

Kula always carried a braided leathern whip about two parthi long (I never saw her without it ... until the morning I slew her). She gave me a cut across the back with it and growled, "Get down there and help her."

I dropped into the pit and took the crank from the girl. She relinquished it gladly, giving me a warm, friendly smile—the first I had ever had from a human.

"Turn it slowly and steadily," she said, "and don't let it stop, or it'll burn and you'll catch it from Kula."

I began to turn. "Like this?"

She nodded. "That's fine."

There was silence for a while. Then she asked, "What's your name?"

"Godranec."

"Mine's Rua." She showed none of the revulsion that the other thralls had shown toward me, and my heart warmed toward her at once.

"Of what people are you?" she asked. "I've never seen anybody like you."

"I don't quite know," I replied. "I have an early memory of a flowery vale in the mountains of the north. Where this vale is, or even if it exists, I don't know."

"I am from an island in the west. Slavers brought me to Chalkhrondu a few years ago and I wound up here."

She was wistful and I wanted very much to comfort her. I kept turning the spit and we kept talking and in a few short minutes we were as friendly as if we had known each other for years.

Then Kula abruptly appeared, and snapped, "Come up here, Rua . . . I don't need the both of you down there."

Rua let her hand rest on my shoulder for an instant . . . a wonderfully warm gesture. I covered it with my own; then she clambered out of the pit.

I turned the crank and watched. Rua was led to the sink where there was a mountain of dirty dishes.

"Wash 'em, you little slut," Kula ordered. "I want to see my face in 'em."

If you see YOUR face in them, I said to myself, *you'll smash them for sure.* Aloud, I said nothing. Turning the spit was easy for me, for though I was not quite as tall as a human boy of my age, I was a good deal more muscular.

I kept watching Rua. Where was this island she

had come from? She was a good deal darker than other humans I had seen. Also, she had not been eating too well. Her eyes showed fear. I wondered why.

Then I found out why.

Rua hadn't been washing dishes long when a large platter, too heavy for her soapy hands to hold onto, dropped against the flagstones of the floor and smashed.

At once, Kula, roaring like a chonglu cat, was on her like a demented thing. The whip smashed against the little girl, every blow drawing blood.

"I told you to be careful," Kula bawled. "I'll teach you to break dishes in here!"

"Don't beat me, vlana!" screamed the girl. "I didn't mean to break it!"

"I'll beat you to death, you little bitch!" roared the cook, and beat the girl harder than ever.

Rua, in despair, seized a butcher knife to defend herself. It was in vain. I couldn't have stood against that great beast. Rua, small and frail, was easily disarmed and dragged shrieking to the door. I watched in horror, unable to interfere, for a guard with a spear appeared above me.

Just inside the door was a large butcher's block where meat was carved for the table. Several carving instruments were in a rack just above it.

Pinioning the screaming girl against the block with her heavy body, Kula put the girl's hands together and held them on the block with her left hand. Then, seizing a heavy cleaver from the rack, she calmly chopped the little girl's hands off at the wrists.

Then, carrying the shrieking, bleeding little wretch by the back of her neck, Kula flung her outside and threw the waxy-white little hands after her. I could still feel where one of them had touched me in friendship, and would feel it until my dying day. It was the first unfeigned friendship I had ever experienced in my life. Rua struggled to her feet and staggered around, shrieking for help that never came, until, weak from loss of blood, she fell to the ground and writhed there, her cries growing fainter until they ceased and she moved no more.

There was the odor of burning meat. I had stopped to watch the horrible sight and the meat had begun to burn. At once Kula was on me. She loved to wield that stiff but strangely flexible whip, and she made my back raw with it. It was absolutely infuriating to her that I refused to cry out. After that, I got the whip every day no matter what I did, but she failed to break me. Thus was born my first real hate. The cold-blooded brutality of the murder of Rua, the only human who had been kind to me, infuriated me. I never allowed my fury to show on my face, but I suspect that Kula read it in my eyes. I had acquired a thing that served to sustain and nurture me in my thralldom . . . a cold fury against humans who would enthrall a helpless little girl then slay her in such a brutal way. I resolved firmly to cut Kula's fat throat sooner or later. It would have to be done carefully, though, so I could get away and find my way back to my own people. I was not yet old enough, nor strong enough, for such a deed . . . besides which, I hadn't the knowledge necessary to make an escape. So I worked, endured, hated, and bided my time.

2

I bore atrocities for five long years,
my meat well-seasoned by my silent tears.
Then Lord Bdengi came to ease my lot . . .
and make my thralldom pleasanter—somewhat.
                                          —The Song of Godranec

As the dilatory years crawled slowly by, my back acquired scars from Kula's whip that I will carry to my grave.

One day, I was sitting on the edge of the roasting pit waiting for the meat to be put on the fire. The fire had burned down to hot coals and was just right for the roasting. Thralls at a large table were inserting the spit into a medium-sized tharg. Suddenly, Kula appeared above me, drunk . . . as usual.

"I hate you, you little animal!" she raved. "I'll break you if it's the last thing I do."

At her sign, a couple of guards seized me and bore me, struggling, to a sturdy table where they held me belly down. I had been forbidden to wear my doublet indoors so my back was bare, as usual.

Kula took a great draft of cooking wine from a bottle she always carried and set it on a nearby table, pushed the sleeve back from her beefy arm, and began to wield the whip with all her considerable strength.

I squirmed from the fire in my back but was determined not to make a sound if she killed me . . . I refused to yield her that satisfaction.

It was likely that she would have beaten me to death . . . but suddenly the Lord Bdengi loomed behind her. He seized the whip, gave her a vicious cut across the face with it, and flung it across the kitchen. He caught one guard across the side of the head and knocked him down and the others let go of me abruptly.

"What in the name of Khanophet are you trying to do?" he roared. "Kill him?"

"What does it matter," Kula growled, wiping the blood from her face with a dirty dish towel. "What good is he?"

"He belongs to me, not to you, you bitch. You've been killing too many slaves down here. Any more of it and I'll take off your own head." He turned to me. "Are you all right, Godranec?"

"Yes, vlan," I said. "Nyarlethim are hard to kill." I threw her a look of pure poison. "And vlan, though it cost me my head to say it, someday I'll get the opportunity I pray for, and by all the gods of the underworld, I'm going to cut Kula's filthy throat!" I almost shrieked it.

"If you don't, I will," he said grimly. "Come along. I've other work for you."

I grabbed my doublet (but didn't dare put it on because of my bleeding back) and went with Bdengi, happy to be out of that place of horror. We passed the bare place outside the door where Rua's blood still darkened the bare earth.

We stopped at the dispensary, where Bdengi ordered the thrall in charge to put ointment on my back and dress it. Then we went to my room for my "things," which filled a very small bundle.

Without speaking, Bdengi led me down to the banks of the Volsek, where a small, neat stone hut stood at the edge of a great meadow, only a few steps from the edge of the wierwoods. This was a haunted forest (or so the humans believed) and no human would go near it under any circumstances.

Bdengi thrust the door open and we entered. I saw a comfortable room with a large fieldstone fireplace with an oven built into one side and a couple of swinging hooks for pots. It had a roughhewn but comfortable bed tucked away in the chimney corner, which would mean warm sleeping at night. There was a table, a lamp, a wooden locker for clothing, and another for food. I saw an earthenware jug in the corner which I supposed held oil for the lamp. It was much larger than my little room at the big house and a great deal more comfortable. It was a little over half a zark* across the meadow from the the smeltery from which Bdengi derived most of his money.

He spoke for the first time since we had left the big house.

"This hut is warm and comfortable," he said, "but I can't get anybody to live here because it's too close to the wierwoods. Would you fear to dwell here?"

"No vlan, I would not."

"They say that savage creatures come out of the wierwoods at night."

I looked at him levelly and said, "Vlan, I have slaved in your kitchen for five weary years. The wierwoods couldn't possibly hold anything more savage than Kula."

He smiled drily. "Perhaps you're right. Can you keep awake at night?"

"Yes, vlan. I like the night better than the day."

"Oh? Why?"

"Because it is peaceful and those who would hurt me are asleep. The only things wakeful are the skarls, the shadow-people who are the children of Shubala, the lord of silences. They are more friendly than the children of men, and are my brethren . . . I fear them not."

"I see. Well, there are things at the plant that must be seen to at night. Of course, the plant doesn't operate at night, but some of the machines

* About a mile, Earth (more or less).

can't be shut off entirely. I have stationed thralls there at night but they always go to sleep, and some expensive equipment has been ruined. You'll be able to sleep during the day and go to work at sunset. What do you say to that?"

"I like it well, vlan."

"You'll be able to prepare your own food right here and you won't have to go to the big house at all."

"I'd like that even better, vlan."

"I'll arrange for you to pick up your rations at the plant. Now come along and I'll show you what you have to do."

I discovered that the Chalkhrondi are an odd mixture of scientific advancement and backwardness. They had some very advanced machinery, which existed alongside of oil lamps. The machines were all manufactured and maintained by engineers from Milar because the Milarians needed the mineral wealth of Chalkhrondu but interfered with the Chalkhrondi as little as possible.

At the time, I never questioned anything as I approached the plant, which was a huge, rambling structure located where the Gelsan canal empties into the Volsek River. The canal had been dug in order to connect the Volsek with the Brogi River a little to the east. Barges, propelled by Milarian machinery, came down the Brogi filled with raw materials from the northern hills (so I was told later). Most cities in Chalkhrondu were built where rivers meet, but Gelsan had been built upriver from the junction because it was a manufacturing center and there were quantities of iron ore found there, as well as a field of natural gas which had been tapped by Milarian engineers and was used for smelting the ore in the making of steel. (Any other use for the substance didn't dawn on the backward Chalkhrondi.) Bdengi's plant made steel products known far beyond the confines of Chalkhrondu, and it had its own docks on the canal. There were no docks on the Volsek because the river plunged directly into the haunted forest just above Bdengi's plant and men feared to go there.

We entered the plant by a door on the river side and I found myself in the office. Bdengi went directly to a large, cluttered desk and began to rummage through some papers. Forgotten for a while, I wandered over to a side table where there was a large drawing of some metal work. I began to spell out the runes written on it.

Presently Bdengi came up and looked over my shoulder.

"You look like you're reading, Godranec," he said.

"I am reading, vlan." I looked up at him.

"Who taught you to read?"

"One of the maids when I was little . . . before I got misshapen and ugly."

"Mmm, you may be more useful to me than I thought. If I were to write special instructions and stick them on this nail by the door, could you read them and carry them out?"

"Yes, vlan . . . if you don't use big words."

"Then it shall be so. Come. I'll show you what to do."

The plant was even more cavernous inside than it looked on the outside. The office was in the southwestern corner of the building. To the left as you entered the plant from the office was a huge wooden rack, some six parthi high,* on which was stored a large quantity of iron rods of various sizes from which tools and other things were fashioned. This rack went all the way to the north end of the building, where a line of forges was located. Behind this rack on the east, various metals in ingot form were piled up. Behind this the stone floor ended and there was a broad bed of clay where molds were buried to make castings of different sorts.

Over the clay bed was a ladle running on an overhead trolley for the pouring of molten steel into molds. The ladle was filled from spouts thrusting from the furnaces in the east room. There were three of these, fired by gas from the field below the plant.

There were some twenty forges in a line along the north wall of the plant. An annex built onto the main building housed special blowers imported from Milar. The forges were fueled with dloth, a soft, porous, oily black substance which burned

---

* *parthu*: A parthu is about sixteen inches, Earth.

fiercely and which was imported from the northern hills. Naturally, much of this information I learned later, but I insert it here to make my narrative more comprehensible.

I was taken to the blower room behind the forges and shown a dial, much like that of a timepiece except that it was larger and had a different system of numbers. About halfway around the dial, a red line was painted on the glass.

"Now, not much can happen here, Godranec," said Bdengi, "but even when the forges aren't operating, this machine can't be shut off completely so long as the flame stones that power it are in the combustion chamber. It's dangerous to remove them until they're used up.

"When you make your rounds, notice the position of this pointer." He indicated the single hand with his finger. "If it is near or on the red line, turn this wheel slightly to the left." He demonstrated. "Understand?"

"Yes, vlan."

"Then stand and watch it for a while. If it doesn't respond to the wheel, then go over to that wall and pull the red lever you see. That will activate a signal that will alert Shaun Vordonath"—he indicated a silent Milarian engineer nearby—"and he'll come down and see what the trouble is. Understand?"

"Yes, vlan."

There were other dials in other parts of the plant

which had to be within a certain range, and I was instructed what to do if they weren't.

So I, Godranec the alien, had a job which was more to my liking than turning the spit under Kula's whip. I was more content, though thralldom was getting more and more irksome to me. In my eyes, I had as much worth as humans who looked down their long noses at me and regarded me as alien and ugly. I determined to flee to freedom some day. The problem was, where? I had no answer to that question, so far, so I determined to keep my eyes and ears open and to try to find out what I needed to know to affect my escape.

I made my rounds the third, sixth, and ninth hour of the night, and the rest of the time was my own. I loved it down by the river at night. Humans were in bed, the stars were bright, and at least two of Vilar's moons were always up and shone with an almost effervescent light which filled me with ecstasy. So, in the meadow where none could see, I danced with the skarls, the little crooked shadows that are the children of Shubala, lord of silent places. The music to which we danced was the gentle, silvery piping of the viruloi, the tiny green insects who are themselves the children of Shubala.

I accepted the skarls as a fact of nature, like the shadows of the trees, except that they were mobile. I was surprised, therefore, when one of them sidled up to me one night and a voice formed in my mind.

"Godranec, why do you remain a thrall of the humans?"

I looked toward where the skarl's body would be if it had one, and, instead of answering the question, I said, "I never knew skarls could talk to people."

"We can talk to people but don't . . . very often. There are no humans worth talking to in the first place . . . and nobody but you ever comes here."

"Are you only shadows, as I have heard?"

"No . . . we're as material as you are. The eyes of other creatures can't see us . . . they see only our shadows. I ask again, why do you remain here as a thrall of the humans?"

"Because I don't know where to go. I don't know where my people are or how to get there."

"Your people dwell at the source of the Volsek, in a valley where the river comes from the mountainside."

"A valley?"

"Yes. Do you know of it?"

"There is a dim memory . . ."

"The memory is truth."

"Seeking the source of the Volsek would mean going through the wierwoods."

"There are worse places than the wierwoods."

"I think you may be right . . . Bdengi's kitchen, for one thing. However, at present, my situation is pretty good. Besides, if I'm to escape I must have weapons and make plans. If I try, and they catch me, they'll skin me alive."

The skarl went to join the others and they began to dance silently again while I got up to make my rounds.

If I could believe him, the skarl had told me where to find my people. I had to have more evidence than that before I would try the wierwoods.

3

The foreman Trinbal, with his one good eye
and rotten teeth in mouth twisted awry,
detested me. His demon eyeball glared . . .
he would have slain me gladly—had he dared.
                                    —The Song of Godranec

As I grew older my sense of alienness increased, as did my desire for freedom. I was certain that if I were to escape at all, I must needs go through the wierwoods, and for that trip I had to have weapons. Slaves were forbidden to bear weapons, so I would have to make them. From time to time I filched tools from the plant with the idea of making arms for myself, but found that I hadn't the least idea of how to go about it. I kept thinking about it and biding my time. My hatred for the children of men grew with my body, though I was careful to conceal it when I walked among them.

So I grew to full strength. When I neared twenty I had almost four times the strength of an adult human male packed in a frame only a little more than half as large. This gave me a nimbleness of foot that would have been astounding to my owner had he seen me dancing in the moonlight. He would have thought me possessed by one of the demon lords who are servants of Khanophet, lord of the underworld.

With the tools I had filched, I made myself many things for my hut, for it gave me pleasure to work with my hands. Unconsciously, I was also training myself in the manipulation of tools. Being untaught, my fancy was unfettered, and the things I fashioned were fantastic but beautiful and I had never seen anything like them in the houses of the humans.

Also, as I grew older, I discovered that my horns had a utility I had never dreamed of. By the time I was full grown they were almost twice as long as my middle finger and were a glossy black.

Their utility was pointed out to me one night as I was resting from my dancing before going on my rounds at the plant. I was sitting on a fallen log near the door to my hut, facing away from the forest. Suddenly, my horns began to tingle and I had an overpowering sense of not being alone.

Being careful not to make a sudden move, I turned slowly, and there, not a dozen paces away, were two of the fabled Halzhengim . . . the lizardmen. These creatures dwelt in the wierwoods and there were a million stories about them. Nothing was actually known of them because humans who had seen them never lived long enough to tell of it. Now here were two of them regarding me solemnly with their great, slit-pupiled eyes.

They were about eight parthi tall and walked upright like humans, balancing themselves by means of their long tails. Their forelegs were like human arms, except that they were covered with scales and terminated in hands quite as flexible and utilitarian as human hands, and they had opposed thumbs. Their heads were a strange mixture of the human and the saurian. I couldn't tell the color of their eyes, for they glowed red with reflected moonlight (as my own were probably doing). Their hands had long fingers terminating in long sharp talons, as did their toes. Fingers and toes were webbed to the last joint, showing that they were amphibian.

After a while, the largest of them spoke in a strange hissing accent, speaking the common tongue with difficulty as if it were alien to him.

"We kill humans . . . you no look human."

"I'm not," I replied.

"What are you?"

"I'm a Nyarlethu . . . so I've been told."

"You look like Nyarlethu. What you do here?"

"Someone—or something—brought me here when I was a baby and I've not been able to get back home again. I'm not even sure where my home is."

"You thrall to humans?"

"Yes."

"Why you no run away?"

"Where to? The skarls said my people live in the northern mountains where the Volsek comes out of the mountainside. I don't know if I should believe them or not. So far I've not been able to get hold of weapons, and I'll need them to get through the wierwoods."

"Hmmm," he said thoughtfully. "That strange story. We enemies of humans but not enemies of you. You see us again."

"That's good . . . I'll need all the friends I can get."

"Not friends . . . not enemies either. We no make friends easy with other races. Must think about story and talk to shogan. If friends, we let you know."

Without another word they turned and melted silently back into the forest. A human would have had a purple frothgar* fit, but I felt oddly invigorated. Maybe I'd be able to escape after all.

Sometimes in the afternoons I awoke early. Then I would fix something to eat and go to the plant, where I would wander about, being careful not to get in the way, and watch the thralls working the forges. For some reason that I couldn't understand I was drawn to the forge and I longed to know

---

* Purple *frothgar*: A vicious narcotic that causes a frenzy and makes the skin temporarily turn purple.

more of the working of metals. The other thralls eyed me askance but said nothing.

Trinbal, the foreman, glared at me with his demon eye (he had lost the other in a drunken brawl). He growled at me but said nothing either for good or bad.

By simply watching the smiths, I learned the proper method of heating the iron and how to work it, noting the color the iron had to be before it could be worked. I stored this in my capacious mind. My hands itched to try it but I dared not ask, so I contented myself with watching.

One night, when I was nearing twenty, I was making my rounds when I saw an intricate piece of ironwork on Bdengi's desk which had been marred in the making. Beneath it was a drawing . . . obviously the piece as the customer wanted it.

After checking my dials, I returned to the office and examined the marred piece. Though I had never had any instruction in forging iron, something deep inside my nature told me what was wrong. In my eagerness I disregarded the consequences of failure.

I took the drawing and the marred piece out to the forge. There was no hurry, for I had all night. I added fuel to a forge that was not quite dead and pulled the lever that turned on the air blast.

When the fire was hot, I put the piece into it with the tongs as I had seen the other thralls do. When my instinct (and my memory of color) told me it was ready, I took it out and, picking up a light hammer, began to work it on the small anvil. I consulted the drawing as the piece was reheating, and it slowly took shape beneath my hands. I added a flourish or two of my own and by the time I had to go on my next round the piece was finished, even more beautifully than the drawing indicated. I cooled it, and, shutting down the forge, I put the piece on Bdengi's desk and went my way.

I thought no more about it.

Late in the afternoon after I had awakened and while I was washing the sleep off me in the basin, Bdengi loomed in the doorway with the piece in his hand.

"Godranec," he said without preamble, "I want to talk to you."

"Yes, vlan?"

"Trinbal marred this piece yesterday and was unable to make it conform to the drawing. I left it on my desk when I went home. This morning it was finished . . . even better than the drawing. Nobody in the plant knows anything about it. That leaves only you. Do you know anything about it?"

"Yes, vlan . . . I did it."

"Where in the unholy name of Khanophet did you learn to do work like this?"

I shrugged. "I watched the others work the metals and last night I tried it. Did I do wrong?"

"No indeed . . . you did exactly right! Here's what I want you to do. I have a thrall who is eager to take the night shift to keep from being slain, for he's too old for anything else . . . fear will keep him awake.

"If you can do work like this with no training, you should be a marvel when you're trained. Take the night off and come to work in the morning and I'll see to it that you're trained."

I made the sign of obedience. "Thank you, vlan . . . I'll be there." I paused, then added, "I did have some trouble reaching the forge."

"I've thought of that. I'm having a platform built around the first forge so you can reach it more easily."

"That takes care of all problems, vlan . . . except one."

"What one?"

"Your people don't like me and I don't have much love for them. The thralls aren't likely to accept my working among them during the day, and I know that Trinbal will persecute me bitterly because I could do what he couldn't. I'm an alien and an outsider, and I'm ugly and misshapen to them."

"I've thought of that too. I don't care much what happens to thralls, for they're not expensive and a whip works marvels on attitudes. Trinbal won't dare touch you, for I've ordered him to lay off you. You're more valuable to me than he is. Satisfied?"

"Yes, vlan. Until tomorrow." I bowed deeply as Vlan Bdengi took his leave.

4

Now, though I was a thrall and he was free,
yet Trinbal kept on persecuting me.
But when he tried to slay, I dared rebel
and sent him to Khanophet's lowest hell.
　　　　　　　　　—The Song of Godranec

When I showed up the next morning at the plant, the other thralls eyed me surreptitiously but said nothing. One or two of them even smiled at me . . . and I smiled back. This wasn't going to be so bad after all. I was turned over to a highly skilled thrall by the name of Khàrkor to be trained in the art of the smithy. A platform had been rigged on the first forge and I could reach it very easily. I soon earned Kharkor's acceptance because of my eagerness to learn, the retentiveness of my mind, and my natural talent for working metal.

In the midmorning my horns began to tingle. I looked around to see Trinbal, hands on hips, glaring at me with his demon eye. Trinbal, I discovered, had a love for displaying his knowledge of epithets in the old tongue. I kept hammering away on the ornamental hinge I was making.

I put the hinge back into the forge to heat, and Trinbal spoke.

"So, the zhenganu [half man] thinks he's a smith."

My grip tightened on the hammer but I made no reply.

"You don't speak to me, snerg?" (A snerg is a small, ugly black ape that lives in the wierwoods.)

"I'm a thrall, vlan," I replied with a great deal more calm than I felt. "I'm supposed to speak to a free man only when spoken to or when I am asked a question."

Trinbal sneered. "Bdengi ordered me to lay off you, and I will. But watch yourself, zahlanglo [ironhead]. You get out of line, even once, and I'll make you wish you'd never been born. Understand?"

"Yes, vlan."

Not being able to get a rise out of me, he stomped off, muttering in his beard.

After a while, Kharkor said, "Trinbal hates all of us thralls, but he seems to hate you most of all, Godranec. Why is that?"

"Because I did something that he couldn't do."

"Oh . . . that ornament."

"I saw it on Bdengi's desk and thought I could

fix it . . . and I did. Bdengi found out who did it, and here I am."

"The other thralls will think better of you now."

"Oh? Why?"

"We like anybody that Trinbal haṭes. I'd keep out of his way, though."

"I'd like nothing better, but how can I? Vlan Bdengi put me here and here I'll have to stay until he puts me somewhere else, Trinbal or no Trinbal."

Nothing more was said on the matter.

At night, too weary to dance in the moonlight with the skarls, I cooked supper in my fireplace, and after a couple of cups of wine (furnished me by Bdengi), I crawled wearily into bed and slept dreamlessly until the morning horn called me to another day. I took a dip in the river, broke my fast, packed a little food for my nooning, and went to work.

On the whole, I would have been happy enough, were it not for the surreptitious but persistent persecution of Trinbal. He kept hammering at me but never dared push it too far for fear of arousing Bdengi's wrath . . . something that was by no means hard to do.

One day when I was beating out an intricate piece of ironwork on the small anvil, Trinbal was evil-saying me as usual and stood too close to the anvil. A chance spark set his greasy tunic on fire.

Cursing like a fiend, he beat out the flames with his hands. Then, seizing a wooden staff which was leaning against a nearby post, he began to beat me savagely across the back.

Aware of the consequences if I were to knock out his filthy brains with the hammer, as I was minded to do, I dropped the hammer and rolled myself into a ball to protect my vital organs and let him beat away . . . there was nothing else I could do.

Suddenly Bdengi loomed up behind Trinbal, snatched the staff out of his hand, and threw it across the shop. He caught Trinbal with his open palm on the side of his head and sent him about six parthi away.

Trinbal clambered dazedly to his feet.

Bdengi roared, "I told you to lay off Godranec."

"Did you see what the little tsolglotz [pile of manure] did? He deliberately set me on fire!"

"Horns of Khanophet! He did no such thing. I saw the whole episode from the door of the office. You've been around forges long enough to know that sparks fly; you should have stood farther away. One more outburst from you and I'll knock your head from your shoulders. Stay away from him. He's a great deal more valuable to me than you are. Understand?"

"Yes, sir."

"Then go about your business."

Bdengi turned to me. I had clambered to my feet, rescued the piece where it was scorching the platform, and put it back on the fire to reheat. I picked up my hammer where I had dropped it and wrinkled my nose at the odor of scorched wood.

"Did he hurt you, Godranec?" he asked me.

"No, vlan . . . I served my apprenticeship under Kula's whip in your kitchen—I'm hard to kill."

"How's the piece coming?"

"If I'm left alone, I'll finish it by nooning."

"If he bothers you, brain him with a hammer. He has no family to raise a fuss and I'll back you if anybody finds out."

I grinned wolfishly. "I would enjoy that, vlan . . . I would enjoy it very much."

He smiled drily. "No doubt you would, at that."

Trinbal was almost pleasant to me after that. He even gave me a grimace or two which was doubtless meant to be a smile. In return, I shot a glance of pure malevolence at him. I do not easily forget wrongs done to me.

Kharkor, at the next forge, snarled under his breath and said, for my ears alone. "Take care, Godranec. When Trinbal smiles he's figured something unpleasant to do to someone."

I shrugged. "Thanks for the warning, but I can't do anything about it but keep on guard."

One day, about midafternoon, Trinbal came up with a genuine smile on his face—which was even more repulsive than his frown, for it displayed his broken, rotten teeth . . . and his breath stank.

"Godranec," he said, using my name for the first time. "Bdengi wants to see you in the office."

My horns tingled—a sign of danger. I took the piece I was working on out of the fire, shut off the blower, and went with Trinbal.

We walked beneath the rack of iron rods . . . just as everyone else did. As we approached the middle of the rack, my horns tingled more than ever. My eyes darted about to see where the danger was—then I saw. One of the main support posts was rotted at the bottom, making it unsafe.

As we passed it, Trinbal looked around to see if anybody was looking . . . then he reached out with his foot and gave the rotten post a vicious kick. The post was knocked from its seat and the rack above began to crack. Warned by my horns, I danced aside like a lightning bolt. (Trinbal had no idea that I could move so fast.) I looked around and saw him looking at me with openmouthed astonishment. I had taken as much as I could take from this dirty, drunken human. The fact that he had planned to murder me by burying me under a dol and a half of iron* made me go berserk. Before he could figure out what I intended to do, I was on him. I picked him up and hurled him, headfirst, halfway across the shop. As he landed he hit his head against a pile of iron ingots, quivered a little, then lay still.

I looked around to see Bdengi behind me.

"I killed him, vlan . . . I'll lose my head over it,

* *dol*: About 2,500 pounds, Earth.

but it was worth it. I should have killed the drunken flokhzotz† weeks ago."

"Well, now, Godranec, I don't think it's as serious as that."

"I slew a free man—that means death."

"Ordinarily it does, but in this case, he has no relatives, so far as I know, so it won't be hard to hush up. There will be an investigation by the police but I'll cover for you and you needn't worry. I think a story that he was drunk and stumbled and hit his head against the ingots will be believed. The police know what a drunk he was."

I frowned up at him. "Why should you cover for me, vlan?"

Bdengi shrugged. "Because you're valuable to me . . . more valuable than he was. As a matter of fact, I fired him a while ago. I'm going to make you foreman in his place."

I looked up at him in astonishment. "Me?"

"Why not? You know more about working metals now than he ever did. I'll replace you at the forge."

"No, vlan . . . not replace."

"Oh? Why not?"

"Because I love to work with metals. I can be foreman and still work the forge . . . at least some of the time."

"Very well, let it be as you will."

In a couple of days the police came around

† *flokhzotz*: Child of unmarried parents—i.e., a bastard.

asking questions. They asked me questions, for they knew how he had been persecuting me. I told them no more than I had to (the Vlan Bdengi coached me in advance), and the other thralls, naturally, told them nothing. Bdengi's story was believed and the incident was closed to everyone's satisfaction, except perhaps to Trinbal's, and he was in no condition to object.

So it was that I, Godranec the alien, became foreman of Bdengi's ironworks and was happier than I had been for years. However, there was still a restlessness in my mind that could not be denied ... a restlessness that demanded to be free.

5

I get a spearhead carved with runic charms,
the lizard-men add to my store of arms.
My lust for freedom mounted when, one day,
Bdengi proved that he had feet of clay.
                    —The Song of Godranec

As foreman, my life was brighter than it had been
in many a year. I was doing work I loved, and the
other thralls forgot their prejudice against me because I was fair and treated them with respect.
Bdengi never objected to this, for it increased pro-
duction, which made him richer. He never interfered with how I ran the shop.

But still, beneath the surface, concealed from all
but myself, was the gnawing lust to be free . . . to
be among people of my own kind. Frequent looks
into the mirror showed me repeatedly the vast difference that separated me from all around me. My
very nature cried out for my own kind. From my

childhood a dim memory had persisted of the flowery vale and the lovely woman of my own kind, she with the soft eyes and gentle hands. The skarl had said that my people lived where the Volsek came out of the mountains. Could I believe him? I had to be sure.

I determined that I would make a break for freedom and began to actively prepare for that day. Nobody ever came to my hut because it was too near the forest. I began to scrounge trash heaps, for the rich people threw away surprisingly good things. I found a pair of sturdy boots that would fit me. One of them was torn a little on the upper but I was clever with my hands and easily repaired it so it was almost as good as new. I oiled them carefully to make them waterproof and put them aside for my trip. Later I found a knapsack that was worn but serviceable. I repaired it, altered it to fit my own form, and put it with the boots. So, slowly, I accumulated equipment.

My main problem was weapons. I knew that the only way to freedom, if I was to avoid the patrol, was through the haunted forest, and I needed potent weapons. This was a major block in my plans.

I found a book in a trash heap that had a picture of a battle-ax in it, a double-bitted affair that looked like it wouldn't be hard to make once I got the opportunity to make a mold. I put the book among my stuff.

My first break came when I was working in the office one day and the chief of police came in carrying a leather-wrapped bundle.

I knew Shalilu by reputation . . . a fat, greasy, wantonly cruel man, proud of his power and eager to use it, especially on the weak and helpless. Bdengi had saved me from his clutches in the case of Trinbal's death.

I appeared to ignore the humans, but my sharp, furry ears swiveled to catch their conversation.

Bdengi had arisen to greet his visitor. "Welcome, Shalilu," he said. "What brings you here?"

Bdengi was never far from a winecup. He offered his visitor one and took another for himself.

"I have a thing here I want you to destroy," said Shalilu. "Here is the court order." He gave an official-looking document to Bdengi.

Bdengi made the sign of respect. "I shall obey the court, naturally. What is it?"

Shalilu unwrapped the bundle with extreme care and displayed a spearpoint some five handsbreadths long and a little less than two handsbreadths wide.

Bdengi took it and turned it over in his hands. "This is a lovely piece of work. Why does the court want it destroyed?"

"As I got the story," said Shalilu after sipping a little wine, "the spearpoint was forged by a wizard. It is supposed to have great power and it always hits what it is hurled at. Nothing can stand before it. There is a spell on it that says it will slay its owner, sooner or later, unless he be 'pure in heart' . . . whatever that means."

Bdengi snorted in derision. "Surely you don't believe that, do you?"

Shalilu shrugged. "I don't know. I do know that that weapon has taken the lives of six high lords . . . seemingly by accident. Its last owner was Kaligari, justice of the high court of Gelsan. His heirs delivered it to me with that court order commanding that it be destroyed."

Bdengi nodded. "The court shall be obeyed." He turned to me. "Here, Godranec, take this out to the furnace room and melt it down. It may as well be part of those tools we're making."

I bowed and took the weapon. "Yes, vlan."

On my way to the back room, I paused between stacks of ingots where none could see me, and I examined the spearpoint. It was truly a graceful and beautiful thing . . . with something of the fearsome in it too. It was sharper than any razor I had ever seen, and it had strange runes scribed into the metal on both sides of it. If they had been put there by a wizard, they must be strong magic. I wouldn't destroy such a weapon—I had use for it. I put it inside my tunic and concealed it in my bundle and took it home with me. Using my filched tools, I fashioned a haft for it, about twice my own height, of hardwood I found at the edge of the forest. At last I had a major weapon for my escape. I oiled it against the damp, wrapped it carefully, and concealed it with my boots and knapsack beneath the floorboards of my hut.

Not long after, not being able to sleep, I was sitting on a stone in front of my cabin in the moonlight when the two (the same two?) lizard-men came out of the forest and advanced to me. My horns weren't tingling, so I knew they were friendly.

The largest said: "We come again . . . see you."

"You are welcome," I said, smiling. "You'll be my friend?"

"Not quite yet . . . not enemy but not friend. Come because you thrall of humans we hate. Bring you word of your people. I learn from shogan, who learn by magic."

I got up excitedly. "Where are they?"

"Where skarls said they were. In valley where the Volsek comes from mountain. Go up Volsek till you can't go farther . . . your people there. Here, you'll need this."

He handed me a sword. It was a beautifully made weapon with a golden hilt set with jewels. It had a finely wrought tempered-steel blade . . . beautifully balanced . . . of the type of steel that holds an edge for a long time. It had a metal, gold-trimmed sheath.

I bowed deeply to the lizard-man and accepted the weapon. "My thanks to you."

"Sword belonged to high lord we catch." There was a sort of grim chuckle. "He not need it now. You escape through wierwoods. Is dangerous but not so dangerous as to go where human patrol catch you. If you live, you come by and by to place where Volsek turns north. Is some sort of great danger there, but shogan not able to find out what. You live, you follow river to where you can't go any more. There your people dwell . . . so says our shogan."

I bowed to him again. "My thanks to you, and take my deepest gratitude to your shogan. May whatever gods you worship give you victory over your enemies."

The Halzhengim lifted their right hands in salutation and melted back into the forest.

Down at the plant, I almost got to thinking that Bdengi loved me, when something happened one day that made me change my mind.

I was working near a forge where Bdengi was watching a thrall by the name of Talu fashion a tool he needed in a hurry. I knew that Talu was ill that day and wasn't equal to the task set him. Halfway through, he erred and the tool was ruined.

With a curse, Bdengi whipped out his dagger and cut the old man's throat. I lowered my eyelids to conceal my anger but said nothing. Other thralls came at Bdengi's call and bore the old man out back and dug a hole and buried him.

So that's the way it is, I thought bitterly. *Bdengi is good to me because I'm valuable to him. Let me make a mistake or lose my value and he'd cut my throat as readily as he cut Talu's throat. I'm getting out as soon as I can. One more thing remains to be done . . . no . . . two more things.*

6

When I had my preparations made,
'twas time to lay a wretched, handless shade.
The butcher butchered, blood for blood repaied,
I vanished in the wierwoods, unafraid.
                    —The Song of Godranec

In one of my rambles among the trash heaps, I picked up a large-scale map of Ghanator. I lugged it home, lit the lamp, and spread it out on the table. I marked the location of Gelsan at the edge of the wierwoods and searched for and found the source of the Volsek in the northern mountains. As I feared, the map was most inaccurate, for it had apparently been based on very sketchy information in the very places I was interested in. I measured the distance with a tape measure I had filched from the shop. How many days would it take? I noticed something written in the margin. I pulled the lamp closer and spelled out the runes. "Exact distances are unknown because the country is entirely unexplored." I made some calculations. It would take . . . at least a year, if, indeed, I should survive at all, for only the gods knew what I should find there. Oh, well, what's the difference? At least my survival would depend on myself and not on the sufferance of humans who would say one thing and do another. I folded the map and put it with my kit.

A few days later, Bdengi called me into the office, where he sat with a number of drawings in front of him.

"Godranec," he said, "Lord Arnoleth has a huge mining operation in the northeastern hills. He mines fire gems such as those that power the machinery out in the shop. His engineers have found a rich vein of them but, because of the peculiarities of the rock in which they lie, he needs special tools to get at them." Bdengi indicated the drawings with a wave of his hand.

"He sent me these specifications and drawings. Do we have the materials necessary to make them?"

I studied the drawings and read the runes describing the quality of the steel. Then I said, "Yes, vlan. We keep everything needed in stock. We were short on vrongeth, but that just came in on the barge a while ago."

"How long would it take to make them?"

"If we start at once and pull men off less important jobs, we could pour this afternoon."

Bdengi nodded. "That's what I figure. We ought to be able to dig out the tools day after tomorrow and finish them."

"Easily, vlan."

"Then let it be done."

I saw in this a golden opportunity to finish the preparations for my escape. That night, when the old thrall who did the watching was out back sitting on a pile of steel where it was cool, I prepared a very special mold and buried it with the others. The workmen wouldn't know how many of the tools there were, and the special mold wouldn't look any different from the top than the others. I would find some excuse to conceal it and dig it up myself after everyone else had gone home.

Everything went as planned. I concealed the special mold, and when the steel had cooled, the men began digging them out. They had a little more than half out when Bdengi came into the shop in midafternoon.

"Stop the work, Godranec. The men must come into the public square."

"Why, vlan?"

"Lord Potrek's thrall who escaped last week has been recaptured. All must come to the square and watch his execution."

"But what of the tools? This will put us behind."

"It can't be helped. Attendance on these affairs is compulsory on all thralls. Come."

A short time later I stood with the other thralls

as the condemned slave, slavering with terror, was dragged to the place of execution. My whole being seethed with indignation, but outwardly I was as calm as if carved from stone.

In the middle of the square, a permanent fixture, was a large, rectangular metal frame bolted to steel posts which were fixed firmly into the pavement. The condemned thrall was dragged to this frame. The guards bound him to the frame, spread-eagled, with one of his limbs lashed to each corner. They ripped the man naked and stepped back.

The slave howled with terror as the executioner, a burly brute with little beady eyes set close to his huge lump of a nose, clothed in black tights below the waist and naked above, strode up with a razor-sharp knife in his hand. A look of intense enjoyment came over his face as he set to work.

The knife babbled in blood and the condemned wretch squalled insanely as his hide was peeled off in large, bloody sheets. Down the line of watching thralls, many were vomiting with horror. I stood like a statue, determined not to let these human beasts see any sign of my inner turmoil.

The condemned man was mad with the agony long before it was over. Even when his hide had been completely peeled away, his muscles twitched still. For a time he kept uttering a soft, mindless ululation, which was more horrible than his shrieking had been.

When he ceased moving, we were marched back to our work.

Back in the shop, Bdengi asked me, "It's almost sunset. Can we get those tools out by tomorrow?"

"Yes, vlan. I'll put the smiths to work finishing those we have out. Those still in the ground I'll dig out and finish tonight after supper."

Bdengi smiled. "You know, Godranec, for a thrall, you're very conscientious."

I shrugged. "Other thralls have it worse than I do. I like to work with metals. It's a good job."

"We have another problem. The old thrall who watches at night died this afternoon of a heart attack and I can't line up anybody else until tomorrow night."

"No problem," I answered. "I'll watch the plant tonight myself."

Bdengi nodded. "Good. Take tomorrow off." He returned to the office.

I was glad of the delay. If all went according to plan, this was my last night in Gelsan.

That night, after digging up and finishing the tools still in the ground (I did this because of my dislike of leaving a task half-finished), I dug up my special mold. I cracked the clay off with a hammer and extracted the beautifully molded head of a battle-ax. The double edges curved gracefully and were a little over a parthu long, and tapered beautifully to the haft-hole. I was alone in the shop when

I heated it and pounded a sharp edge on the blades. I concealed it in my cloak and took it home. Using my tools, I fashioned a hardwood haft for it and had a marvelously crafted weapon which was well balanced and reached about to my shoulders when standing on the ground. The handle and retaining strap were of braided rawhide which I had fashioned previously. Wielded by my powerful muscles, it should be a deadly weapon. As an afterthought, I took a scribing tool I had filched and incised on the ax-head and the sword blade the same runes which were on the spear point. I didn't know their import, for I couldn't read that mode. They had been put there by a wizard, though, so they must be very powerful. For good measure I added the device tattooed on my own left breast. This device was a half-circle and some equally strange runes, plus the initials "S. N." in common runes. I didn't know what they meant either, but they had always been there, and to me they signified ownership, for they were part of my own body. I filled my knapsack with food I had stored up . . . I wouldn't need water since I would be walking beside the river. I rolled up my blanket and tied the ends and lashed it to my pack. Now I was ready for my escape . . . except for one thing.

I set about this task swiftly because Kula was an early riser. I had by no means forgotten the dying shrieks of little Rua after Kula had chopped her hands off. I had seen Rua's shade in dreams on my bed, and fancied I saw her at times in the moonlight at the edge of the forest, seeming to plead for vengeance. Now she would be avenged.

I took up my sword and tested its edge. Sharp—good! It had been made for a human, so it was too long for me to wear at my side. I lashed it across my back, slantwise, so the hilt protruded over my left shoulder within easy reach of my right hand.

Thus armed, I headed for the plant. There, I turned the dials down as far as they would go, then I headed swiftly up the hill to the big house. The weather decided to cooperate with me, for a fog had sprung up from the river which would conceal my actions from any prying eye.

Kula's door was unlocked. I drew my sword and pushed the door open carefully, catching my breath when a hinge squeaked. I looked across the room to the bed where she lay on her back snoring lustily. Silently I approached the bed.

As I bent over the bed, sword in hand, my face twisted with hate, her snores ceased . . . and her eyes flew open. For the first time I saw fear in them. My left hand closed over her mouth to stifle a cry and my right hand drew the sharp sword blade across her throat.

The skin split with the sound of a melon being sliced open and there was a soft hissing sound as the blood gushed from her severed arteries. When the windpipe severed, I snatched a garment, which would be easily recognized as mine, from my belt and thrust it into her dying hands. I didn't want some helpless thrall to be blamed for a deed that I had done. I sawed happily until the head was completely severed and she stopped moving. The beast was dead . . . Rua was avenged. I wiped the sword on the bedclothes and sheathed it.

I left the chamber, closing the door behind me. The fog was already lifting. I trotted quickly downhill to my hut, donned the rest of my equipment, and took the last look around. I had been happier here than I could remember being, but now I would be free.

I blew out my lamp, closed the door behind me for the last time, and, as the first light of dawn bloomed in the east, I disappeared into the wierwoods.

7

Whatever dangers here to threaten me,
I was content, so long as I was free.
I strode on, heedless—drunk on freedom's breath—
but in the wierwoods, carelessness means death.
                              —The Song of Godranec

It should work out nicely, I said to myself. *By the time they miss Kula and somebody investigates and finds her body, I should be deep enough into the wierwoods to be out of reach of the patrol. It isn't likely that they'd come into the woods for any consideration, so I should be safe from them. Are the creatures here as savage as I have heard? They can't be more savage than the humans that have held me in thrall since babyhood. I'll take it as it comes. At least my survival will depend on myself and nobody else. As long as I am free, I am content.*

The river murmured quietly on my left and the woods brooded darkly on my right. At times, the great trees overspread me like a canopy and I walked in dense shadow. I could smell the wet, fishy odor of the river mingled with the exquisite scent of night-blooming flowers from the forest. I began actually to enjoy myself. The feeling of being free was intoxicating.

As it grew lighter, the footpath I was following became more distinct. *Footpath?* The thought suddenly occurred to me. *What sort of creature would make a footpath, here in a place where humans never came?* I didn't really want to know . . . I'd probably find out soon enough. I saw nothing but a few huelgi* nosing about the river bank for worms.

At nooning, I paused on a spit of sand that jutted out into the river, put my back against a rock where I could watch the river and the forest at the same time. I dug some bread and cheese out of my pack and ate sparingly. I drank from the river, which was pure and clean and not at all like the Brogi, which came down from the northeastern hills and was polluted by mud and mine tailings. I was almost finished when I spotted the head of a lizard-man protruding from the water, watching me solemnly. He made no threatening move, so I stared back at him until he ducked beneath the water and disappeared.

After resting, I donned my pack again, picked up my weapons, and resumed my journey. As I traveled, I saw other lizard-people moving from

---

* *huelgu:* A large rodent about three parthi tall at the shoulder. A prime source of meat for predators.

tree to tree, but they made no hostile move and besides, my horns weren't tingling, so I feared nothing from them. What had the Halzhengim said? "Not friends—not enemies either." There were, no doubt, other creatures in the forest more dangerous than they.

At midafternoon my horns *did* began to tingle, which brought me to full alert. My eyes went to the forest instinctively. Were the Halzhengim about to attack me?

Almost too late I caught a flash of scarlet from above and danced aside as the great triangular head of a lilikhanu, a fire-serpent, missed me narrowly.

In the same movement my ax flashed and I sprang aside to avoid a deluge of blood as the great headless, scarlet serpent fell from the overhead branch where it had been awaiting its prey. It threshed violently on the path and I stood to watch it die. The thing was fully fifty paces long and its bright red color had given it its name. It wasn't poisonous but it was large enough to swallow a bigger person than I, whole. Where there was one, there would be another. I washed my ax in the river and dried it in the sand. Then, skirting the still-twitching serpent, I fared onward, keeping watch on the overhead branches as well as the river and the forest.

I encountered no further enemies, and when the sun began to wester I looked for a place to spend the night, for I hadn't had any sleep at all for almost two days. Just before sundown I saw it. The river made a bend to the west and between the bank and the water was a broad stretch of hard-packed sand at least two or three hundred parthi wide. In the center of this expanse of sand was a large, flat-topped rock that must have been at least fifty parthi high and twice that long. If I could only get to the top of that, I should be fairly safe. I went out and circled the rock. About two-thirds of the way around it, I saw a place where it could be climbed. It would be a hard climb for me, but if it was hard for me, it ought to be even more difficult for enemies.

I thrust my spear haft through the lashings of my pack, thus freeing my hands. I hung the ax to my girdle by the retaining strap and began to climb.

For one of my stature, fifty parthi was a long way, and though I was powerfully built and had worked for over a year as a blacksmith, still, before I reached the top of the rock, I discovered muscles that I never knew I had.

Clambering out on top of the rock at last, I laid my weapons down, removed my pack, and stretched out at full length on my back to get my breath. I had a spectacular view of the river and the forest and, from this vantage point, should be able to spot enemies long before they spotted me. I wouldn't be lucky enough to find a place like this every night. What would I do for protection the other nights it would take me to get through the forest? Oh, well, I'd worry about that later. Now, it was enough to be free, to eat a little cold meat and bread. I had drunk my fill from the river earlier. Then, as the sun dipped beneath the horizon and night dropped down on the world, I rolled up in my blanket and went to sleep.

In the early light of dawn I awoke with a start as a great, croaking bellow welled up from below. I fought clear of my blanket and peered cautiously over the edge of the rock. Between me and the river I saw a huge slegoth, without doubt the same carnivorous marine lizard I had seen in the river yesterday—or one like it. It normally ate fish but I knew it wouldn't stick at eating a Nyarlethu, if it could catch me.

It wasn't large enough to reach the top of the rock, and I had lots of food. Water, however, would soon be a problem, and the slegoth could stand a siege longer than I could. I ducked down so it wouldn't see me and considered what to do.

The beast was busily depositing dirty grey eggs, each as long as my arm and about half that wide, in a hole it had dug in the sand with its flippers. I decided to try to get down the rock on the side opposite to the lizard and try to get into the forest before it saw me.

I managed to get down the rock without making noise. I was a little stiff in the muscles after a night on the hard rock, but they loosened up as I used them. I was a little less than halfway to safety when the treacherous breeze shifted and the beast winded me. It had just finished covering its eggs and decided, in its dim saurian brain, that I would make a tasty breakfast. It was after me in an instant.

I discovered that the sand was not packed nearly as hard as I thought, and the slegoth, in spite of its apparent clumsiness, could move with astounding speed. It was closing in on me fast.

Just when I thought I was lost, I came to a large outcropping of bare, flat rock which gave me solid footing. I realized that I couldn't possibly reach the shelter of the trees in time, so I turned at bay.

The lizard's jaws were larger than I was tall, so, distrusting the spear with such a target, I dropped it and gripped my ax in both hands. The great head flashed down on me. I danced aside just far enough to avoid the jaws, and my ax whistled through the air. Unfortunately, the head was moving a little slower than I thought and my ax only cut a large chunk out of the beast's snout.

Roaring with rage and pain, it struck again, allowing for my movement. I figured it would do exactly that, so I moved in the opposite direction. This time my ax thunked solidly into the neck, just behind the head, and cut it part of the way through. The beast, bleeding in rivers, splashed me with gore and struck again and again. I managed just barely to keep out of the reach of its jaws.

Finally, weakened by loss of blood, its recovery

was just slow enough to allow me to dance in. My ax flashed and the head was severed. I sprang backward to avoid the deluge of blood as the beast threshed in its death throes.

I leaned on my ax and panted until I recovered my breath. I feared to stay too long, for the smell of blood would draw predators from a long distance. I drew my sword, skinned some hide off a haunch, and cut myself a huge steak. I knew from experience that lizard meat was good to eat. I got a large leaf from one of the bushes at the edge of the clearing and wrapped my meat in it. I put it in my pack and moved onward, hoping to find a place where it would be safe to build a fire.

As I traveled, I noticed a troop of snergs at the edge of the forest. They paid no attention to me but went about their business of gathering food. I stopped for a little to watch them.

Then I noticed that they picked and ate only certain fruits and herbs and left others alone. I marked the ones they ate and reasoned that anything they ate, I could eat. I picked some of the approved fruits for myself. They were delicious. Here was a new source of food. I decided to keep an eye on my little cousins; I would learn of other things I could eat, for a continuing source of food was beginning to worry me. Now it was solved . . . I could feed off the forest. Now if only I could kill some of the huelgi I would have a supply of meat. They moved awfully fast, though, and would perhaps be hard to hit with a spear.

I kept striding along, almost merrily, picking and eating fruits as I went. The snergs allowed me to glean fruits almost within arm's-length of them, apparently regarding me as just a somewhat larger snerg. (Perhaps Trinbal had been right and I was a snerg after all.)

A little before nooning, I had a rude lesson in how *not* to travel through the wierwoods, when suddenly I blundered into a narbo web. It was an immense web, the strands of which were almost invisible. These webs were supposed to be almost unbreakable, for I had never heard of anybody escaping one. Then I saw it—a huge, hairy, black-and-white spider coming slowly down the web towards me. What could I do? Its body alone was almost three times the size of mine and my movements were hampered by being stuck in the web. I was lost!

8

If one wants to travel wild and free,
a narbo web is not the place to be.
I get help of a most unusual kind—
and afterwards a new companion find.
                    —The Song of Godranec

I knew instinctively that if I threshed about I would
get myself even more hopelessly entangled in the
web, so I fought down my terror and remained absolutely still. I had dropped my ax but my right
arm was free. Working carefully to keep it from
getting entangled too, I reached up to where the
hilt of my sword protruded over my left shoulder
and drew the weapon carefully from its sheath.
Even as I did so, I knew it was hopeless, for the
spider would only shoot additional strands and en-
tangle my sword arm too, and I would be truly
helpless.

Then I heard a roaring sound from above. Cran-
ing my neck, I looked in the direction and saw a

lithikhar, a type of huge black-and-orange-striped wasp. I kept still and watched. I didn't fear the wasp, for I had heard that it never attacked anything but its natural prey, the narbo . . . and that's what it was after now. When the narbo saw its enemy, it froze, then started to retreat. The lithikhar could move a lot faster, and before the spider could escape the wasp dived, a great stinger as long as my whole body extruded, and stabbed the spider with extreme precision and froze it into immobility. The wings of the great wasp beat like thunder as the powerful insect pulled the spider from the web and bore it off, ignoring me entirely.

Now my problem was to get free from the web. My sword was probably hopeless, for I had heard that men had tried to cut a narbo web before and the tough fiber was proof against any edge. The sword or ax would bounce off as if the web were made of tempered steel. The sword was all I had, so I tried it.

Much to my surprise, when the sword rasped across one of the strands, the strand parted with a musical twang. What was this? The sword *did* cut the web. I worked carefully, for even though the sword couldn't be entangled in the web, my arm could. Eventually I got my feet on the ground and a little more work made me free. I managed to get the cut strands off my clothing. I recovered my weapons, sheathed my sword, and retreated to a safe distance to consider.

Why had my sword cut the web when other swords had failed? There was only one explanation. The runes I had inscribed on the blade, copied from the spearhead, evidently had true magical properties . . . there could be no other explanation. The runes had given the sword the properties of the spear. I tried the web with the spear head. It cut the tough fiber like cheese. So did my ax. Now all I had to do was to keep from getting entangled in the webs. Moving the spear up and down in front of me to avoid the almost invisible webs, I resumed my journey.

At nooning I found a good place by the river where there was plenty of driftwood. I knew my lizard steak wouldn't keep long in the heat, so I built a fire and roasted it with some of the salt I had brought along in my pack. It was delicious. After resting I traveled on.

An hour or two past nooning I caught a flash of red from up ahead. Another fire serpent? No. On closer investigation I saw that it was a great chonglu cat caught in another narbo web. I had read of them. They were very powerful, but were supposed to have great intelligence for a wild animal.

A huge spider, even larger than the one that had threatened me, was close to its prey. The cat was watching it with frightened green eyes. The cat was about ten parthi long, without counting its tail, and had a formidable array of claws and teeth, useless to it in a narbo web.

After my recent experience I hated narbethi, so I approached the web carefully. The narbo halted its advance and turned its attention to me. I reasoned that the seat of any intelligence the creature might have would be centered in its relatively tiny brain, which would be situated between its huge compound eyes.

When my spearhead encountered the first strand, I halted. The narbo hissed and sprang at me. I had made my spear-haft extra long for just such emergencies. I held it by the end of the haft and guided the spearhead directly between the eyes of the brute. The charmed steel sank deep. The thing threshed madly with pain and became hopelessly entangled in its own web. I had sprung back as my spear sunk home, and now I waited patiently until the thing stopped moving. I approached carefully and drew my weapon from the body and cleansed it by thrusting it into the ground. Then I turned my attention to the great cat. I couldn't leave it here to starve.

I began to talk to it in a soft voice. Its ears, which had been laid back along its head, now came forward, and the great green eyes seemed to beseech me. After a little, I touched it and began to stroke it behind the ears, something any animal loves. After I had calmed its fears, I took my spear-head and, working carefully to avoid becoming entangled in the web myself, I cut the cat free. I accompanied him as he dragged himself to the river and drank deeply. He lay down on the warm sand to rest, his eyes showing gratitude toward me.

I didn't know how long he had been entangled in the web, but it was obvious that he was weak from his fight against the strands and from lack of food. I saw some huelgi upriver, and the wind was coming my way. I managed to spear one of them, and cut off a foreleg for myself and gave the rest to the cat, whom I named Chong. He ate noisily and gratefully. I washed my meat in the river, wrapped it, and put it in my pack for my supper. The cat regained his strength rapidly, and when I resumed my journey, Chong padded sedately beside me like an immense pet tabby cat.

When night came on, I sought a place where I felt reasonably safe, gathered fruits from nearby bushes, and roasted my huelgu leg and made a very nice supper. Chong disappeared for a while, then reappeared with a small antelope he had caught somewhere. He permitted me to take what I wished and he dined on the rest. We both made camp like the best of companions. It was odd, but the huge carnivore was a great deal more gentle than the humans I had lived among since infancy.

I knew by this time that wild animals are afraid of fire . . . but then, so was Chong. Therefore, in deference to his feelings, I let the fire go out, and when night descended on the world, I rolled up in my battered blanket and slept beside the great cat, his soft, purring warmth a welcome shield against the chill of night. In the morning, we both broke our fast on the remnants of our supper, drank from the river, and resumed our march upriver, my great red friend evidently deciding to accompany me. I was happy of his company, for two of us would be safer against enemies than one of us alone.

As I traveled, I felt myself becoming accustomed to the forest. My body toughened and I felt myself more alert and quick of movement than I had ever been. I kept my weapons ready for instant use, for my life depended on my quickness and alertness. A couple of lizard-men always trailed me, either from the river or from deeper in the forest, but they made no move toward me for either good or ill. I wouldn't worry about them until my horns tingled or they made some sign of hostility. So far they seemed to be merely observing.

We traveled by easy stages, halting when tired, and I kept eating fruits that grew by the wayside, fruits I saw the snergs eating.

The sun had far westered when I came upon a large oblong lake which had a low, rocky island in the center of it. There was not a living thing in sight except the two of us, Chong and I. The scene was peaceful enough, so I made camp at the foot of a bluff, with about three hundred paces between me and the shore of the lake, whose waters murmured peacefully as they washed against the beach. I thought I saw strange-looking ripples out in the

water. What was it? I shrugged . . . possibly fish.
Nothing to worry about.

I built a small cooking fire and roasted the remains of a huelgu I had taken earlier with my
spear. Then, as night descended, I rolled up in my
blanket and went to sleep with Chong purring
peacefully beside me.

In the middle of the night I was awakened by
Chong, growling from deep in his chest. I sat up
and looked around. Three of Vilar's moons were up
and vision was clear. Then I wished I were somewhere else. Coming out of the lake and wriggling
up the shore toward us was a horde of strange creatures. They were an abhorrent mixture of human
and serpent. They had shoulders like a human, and
the first pair of their six short legs were articulated
like human arms, with webbed, taloned powerful-
looking fingers. Their other lizardlike limbs seemed
too small to carry their bodies. They were mottled
all over and were covered with scales—I couldn't
tell what color they were in the moonlight and I
had no intention of letting them get close enough to
me to find out . . . if I could help it.

It was evident that their webbed limbs wouldn't
permit them to move very fast on land, which was
an advantage for me. However, there were hordes
of them and they had already cut off my retreat, so
what to do?

The cliff? It looked smooth; but on closer inspection I saw handholds which made it not too dif-

ficult to climb. Fifteen parthi up there was a broad ledge, which ought to offer at least partial protection if the things couldn't climb any better than they could walk, for it was apparent that they were more at home in the water than on land.

I tossed my pack, blanket, and weapons up on the ledge and started to climb. But . . . what of Chong?

I needn't have worried, for, as I began to climb, the intelligent beast divined what I was up to and gathered his muscles and leaped smoothly to the ledge. I wished that I could jump like that. Instead I had to climb. The first of the creatures were nipping at my heels as I scrambled over the ledge to safety.

Then I wondered how safe the ledge was going to be, for the things were tall enough when standing on their hind legs to reach the ledge with their flat, snaky heads.

I promptly grabbed my ax and began to split the heads as soon as they appeared. Some of the tallest were even able to hook their forelimbs onto the ledge and were beginning to try to pull thmselves up when I started to slice the heads off the things. I had a constant battle of it for the rest of the night, but I managed to keep them off the ledge. The things were evidently poisonous for they had long fangs. They were also of limited intelligence for there was no cooperation among them and no evidence of planning. Chong wasn't idle either. He was immensely powerful and a sweep of his mighty paw would knock off the head of a serpent-man . . . so, between us, we did very well for ourselves.

Then there was another problem. The creatures started to come faster and seemed to be having an easier time reaching the edge of the ledge. A glance below showed that they were mounting the bodies of their slain. Chong and I stepped up our efforts, but the sheer numbers of the creatures would overwhelm us soon.

Slowly and imperceptibly during the battle, the night faded into dawn. Chong and I were battling bravely against mounting odds when the first rays of Vilar's double sun spilled over the edge of the world.

At once there came a hissing cry from the lakeshore. Abruptly the serpent-men broke off the battle, retreated to the edge of the lake, and slipped beneath the waves. It was evident that they were nocturnal and couldn't stand the light of day.

When they had vanished, I saw that the piled-up bodies of the serpent-men were almost halfway up the cliff. It would be unpleasant to jump down on them, but I saw no alternative, for I couldn't climb the cliff any farther. I donned my equipment and sprang down to the pile of bodies and scrambled down to solid ground. I made my way up the lake shore with all possible speed to put as much distance as possible between myself and the serpent-men. Chong was right beside me.

The bluffs continued, sometimes close and sometimes far. I also noted that they were honeycombed with caves. Maybe I could hole up in a cave for sleeping if I could find one that was not occupied by some noxious creature.

When I was a safe distance from the lake, I paused to break my fast on fruits from my pack and the remnants of my bread and cheese. Chong had dined earlier on one of the dead serpent-men. My stomach was not exactly weak, but it demanded daintier fare than that. I was bone-weary and sleepy—but did I dare sleep?

Then the thought occurred to me. With my slit-pupiled eyes, I could see in the night quite as well as in the day. The predatory creatures I had to fear were obviously nocturnal. If I slept during the day, I would encounter them at night when I was alert and wakeful, which would be better than to have them sneak up on me when I was asleep. If Chong hadn't warned me, I would have been dead . . . and how much longer would he stay with me? Not long, I feared. I therefore found a cave that wasn't too accessible, and one that was too shallow to have dangerous beasts farther back. Chong and I holed up in that and slept for the rest of the day, I on a pile of grass which I had gathered in the vicinity. It was most comfortable.

When I awoke at evening, Chong, who had arisen earlier, was returning with a huelgu he had caught. After I washed the sleep off me in the river,

Chong yielded me a piece of a haunch and I roasted it over a small fire. Then, after dining, we two oddly assorted companions continued on our journey.

9

I'm caught between hereditary foes,
and Chong decides he's had enough and goes.
I meet an one who unto me communes
the hidden meaning of the mystic runes.
                              —The Song of Godranec

A couple of nights later, about midnight, I was striding along rapidly and making good time. The cliffs were about five hundred paces to my right (and not very high here), and the river about another hundred paces to my left. The moons were very bright and I could see as well as in the day.

All at once I heard a sound as of thousands of clawed feet moving on the sand, and from the river came a great wave of lizards. They were a type of lizard I had never seen before. They came about to my waist in height and were about five to eight parthi long. It was obvious that they were carnivorous and that they ran in packs like wolves. They had winded me and were determined to pull me down and make a meal of me. Chong saw them as soon as I did. He spat and yowled, then made for the cliffs, which he cleared in three bounds, and disappeared into the forest. I never saw him more.

What was I to do? They were very fast on their feet and I couldn't outrun them, but I could damned well try. I took to my heels.

A glance behind me showed that they were gaining on me. I despaired of escaping. Then I saw an immense dead tree not far away. About thirty parthi up there was a place where the huge branches came together. If I could get up there I could make a stand, for they could only come at me a couple at a time. Could I do it?

I never could figure out how I climbed that tree, but fear makes a person do impossible things. The next thing I knew I was up in the fork of the tree. The tree was dry and leafless so I could see . . . a great deal more than I wanted to see. The quarters were too crowded to use my ax, so I stuck it in the tree where it would be handy and drew my sword.

The things began to climb, clumsily because of their weight. I began to hack at saurian heads as soon as they came within reach. The dead ones fell and knocked others from their hold farther down the trunk. I stood my ground—I had no choice— wondering how long I could hold out, for there seemed to be hundreds of the things.

Then there came a hissing scream from a small hill farther east towards the cliffs. The lizards halted their tree-climbing, their forked tongues shot in and out questioningly, then they scrambled down the tree again. As one, the whole horde faced the cliffs. I followed the direction of their gaze and saw an astounding sight.

From the caves an army of huge scorpions were coming. The insects were at least five parthi long and they stood at least two parthi high. They had long tails with venomous stings on the tip. I saw no escape, for the scorpions could climb the tree even more rapidly than the lizards could and they were far more agile.

The lizards had forgotten all about me, and it was increasingly apparent that the lizards and the huge insects were hereditary enemies.

Then there ensued the strangest battle I had ever heard of. The two armies clashed together and there was a bitter fight without quarter. Slashing jaws would wound a scorpion to the death, but the stings of the insects almost always went home. The screaming of the lizards was unnerving. The whole plain was a tangle of fighting, heaving bodies. From observation, I guessed that the insects were shortsighted, so I remained absolutely motionless in my tree so as not to attract their attention. They couldn't wind me so high above the ground.

The scorpions won the battle because of superior weapons. The few surviving lizards scrambled for the river and managed to escape in the concealing waters. The victorious insects dragged the corpses of their victims back to their caves for a feast. Soon the plain was empty again.

When it seemed safe to do so, I descended from my perch, almost breaking my neck in the process. How in the name of Khanophet did I ever get up there?

Needless to say, I legged it upriver as fast as I could go before the scorpions winded me and came to investigate. I missed Chong but couldn't blame him for running away.

I was thinking of the big cat, and my mind wasn't on what I was doing. I had slowed to a walk when suddenly, from a clump of bushes, a lizard roared out at me. It had been badly wounded but was still full of fight. I danced aside and split its head with my ax, but not before its teeth had laid my thigh open.

I looked around for another but saw nothing. The moonlight made tricky shadows. Of necessity, I paused, tore a strip from the hem of my cloak, and bound up the wound on my thigh as best I could. It was pretty bad and would give me trouble. The lizard hadn't been poisonous but its teeth had been far from clean. With my leg bound as well as I could, I struggled to get a safe distance beyond the scorpions' caves. How many other colonies of the things would there be? Oh, well, so long as I was free, I'd fight on until I dropped.

The Vilarian double sun was well above the horizon before I felt myself safe enough to pause. I was looking for a good place, with my leg bothering me more and more. (Did I have a fever?)

I was approaching a number of huge flowers with great purple blossoms when my horns began to tingle and I paused to sort things out.

It was fortunate that I did, for one of the blossoms turned toward me and shot a jet of almost invisible vapor at me. Instinctively I retreated with as much speed as I could muster. I got the merest whiff of the stuff, and the rich, intoxicating odor seemed to beckon me toward the flower so I could get more of the sweet odor. My head swam. I hadn't breathed much of the stuff, though, so by an effort of will I remained where I was until the feeling passed. Then I saw it.

At the edge of the path, one of the huge plants had something wrapped tightly in its bright green leaves—the blossom itself closed over the head of the victim. On close inspection (from a safe distance), I saw that the victim was a human—a female, for part of her stuck out of the tightly wrapped leaves. I had no reason to love humans (quite the contrary), but it seemed a vile thing to leave without doing something to help her, for a quiver of her foot showed that she was alive.

The problem was, how could I help her without falling victim to the things myself? Then the thought occurred to me that it was the almost invisible vapor that did the trick. If I could move fast enough and cut the thing down, holding my breath the while so I wouldn't breathe the vapor, I ought to be able to bring it off.

I rid myself of my pack and everything that might hamper my movements. Then, gripping my ax and taking a deep breath, I held it, dashed in, and severed the thing with a single stroke of my ax just above the ground. I dashed to safety again before daring to breathe again.

Then I looked back. I saw the plant writhing on the path like a beheaded serpent, bleeding a stinking green sap. Other plants were writhing as if in sympathetic pain, their blossoms turning this way and that as if trying to locate the source of the danger.

The woman had been thrown onto the path not far away . . . she seemed unconscious. Holding my breath again, I dashed in, grabbed her by the arms, and dragged her a safe distance from the plants. Then I examined her curiously.

I had never seen her like before. She was obviously not Chalkhrondu so I felt more kindly toward her. She was extraordinarily tall for a woman and much darker than any human I had ever seen before. She was very thin for her height and her aquiline features showed her definitely not of any race I had ever seen. Her age was uncertain—at least she was one of those people who don't show age. I took a battered tin pan from my pack and brought some water from the river and bathed her face with it.

Soon she began to stir . . . then her large eyes came open. They were a vivid, almost startling grey—further proof that she wasn't Chalkhrondu, for Chalkhrondi have black eyes. I supported her head on my arm and gave her to drink.

Her eyes were blank at first, then suddenly they focused and she spoke.

"Who are you?" she asked in a musical contralto.

"I am Godranec the alien," I said.

"Alien?"

"Yes, my lady."

"Why alien?"

"Because I am different from any that I have ever seen. I hear there are people like me in the mountains of the north, but I have never seen them. I go there to seek them now."

She passed the back of her hand across her eyes as if in puzzlement. "What day is this?"

"I've more or less lost track of time, but I think it's the fourteenth day of the fifth month of the Year of the Turtle, my lady."

"I've been trapped in that thing for almost a week. You rescued me. My thanks to you. A little longer and it would have sapped my life-force. As it is, I don't think I can get up."

"How came you to be trapped by those things?" I asked.

"I'm a spaewoman from the western ranges of the forest, and they don't grow there. By the time I realized my danger it was too late and I was trapped. How came you to escape them?"

"I'm not human, my lady," I replied. "My horns tingle when I'm in danger. I saw the vapor and dodged it."

Her gaze had been roaming curiously over me. Suddenly it focused on my leg.

"You're wounded?"

"There's a large type of carnivorous lizard just south of here. I had a fight with one and he almost got me."

"It should be treated."

"I know that, but I don't know how."

"I do." Her eyes were searching the edge of the forest.

"Look over there," she said. "See that bush with the large, bright-orange fruits on it?"

"Yes, my lady. I've not been picking them, for I didn't see the snergs eating them and thought they would be poisonous."

"You've been eating things you saw the snergs eat?"

"Yes, my lady; it seemed wise."

"It was. However, the snergs don't eat those because they can't get through the rind. Go pick some and bring them to me."

I did as she ordered and was soon back with a lapful of the fruit, which were a little prickly and had a tough rind. They were about the size of my fist. I gave them to her. I helped her sit up and she leaned her back against a tree at the edge of the path.

"Split a couple of them open for me, please," she said.

I split a half-dozen open with my sword. She took one of the cut fruits, tipped it to her mouth, and sucked the juice from the pulp. The change in her was amazing. After drinking the juice of three of the fruits she was able to get to her feet. After walking up and down a bit to get back her strength, she bent over me.

"Lie down," she said, "and let me look at that leg."

She removed the rough, blood-soaked bandage from my wound. It was feverish and I was beginning to get giddy from it.

"That's a bad wound," she said, "but I can fix it."

She took one of the cut fruits and, holding it over the wound, squeezed the juice into it. At once a grateful coolness spread through the fevered flesh and the bleeding stopped. After the juice of three of the fruits had been squeezed into it, the wound lost its angry redness and the swelling had gone down. She bandaged it with a strip torn from her petticoat.

"When in the forest," she said, "keep an eye out for these fruits and carry some in your pack. They have great medicinal value and can restore you when weary as nothing else in existence. They grow all over the forest. You don't have anything to eat, do you? I'm starved after a week in that thing."

"I'm afraid I don't," I said. "But let's go back down the path a little to get away from those devil-flowers, and we can camp by the river. I should be able to spear a huelgu and we'll dine."

"Sounds good," she said. "Let me lean on your arm a little . . . I'm still pretty weak."

Her hand was cool and firm on my arm as I led her back down the path to a good spot by the river where I could see enemies long before they saw me. I left her there, slipped upwind, and speared a huelgu. Shalilu had been right, evidently, for the spear never missed and I knew I wasn't *that* good with it. I had some difficulty, as I always did, in skinning the thing with the spearpoint for I had no knife and the sword was much too clumsy for the purpose. I managed, however, and, bearing the meat back wrapped in a bundle of leaves, I built a fire using my flint and the edge of my ax. I roasted the meat with a little of my carefully hoarded store of salt, and the spaewoman (whose named was Mlada) and I made quite a good meal. Our conversation was sweet, for I had become very lonely with none for company but myself.

As we talked, her bright gaze fixed on my ax, which was lying between us, and she saw the runes I had carved there.

"Where did you get that ax, Godranec?"

"I made it. I was thrall to a smith in Gelsan."

"And the runes?"

"Copied from the spearhead, which was made by a wizard."

I passed the spear over and she examined the runes with great interest.

"Can you read them?" I asked.

"I can."

"They must be great magic," I said, "for ax, spear, and sword cut a narbo web as if it were wool."

"They are great magic," she replied. "But these other runes here by the crescent are just as strong . . . though they are in a different mode than the other. How came you by those runes?"

"It signifies ownership to me."

"How so?"

"I bear the device on my own person."

Her luminous gaze bent on me with almost hypnotic intensity. "Am I permitted to see?"

I shrugged. "If you like." I pulled my ragged shirt aside and showed her the mark tattooed on my left breast above my heart.

The wonder in her face deepened. "How came you by that mark?"

I shrugged. "It has always been there. Is it important?"

"Indeed it is. Look you." With the end of her finger she traced three words in letters of the common tongue. "Can you read that?"

"Yes, my lady. It says—"

She lifted her hand. "Speak them not, but hold them in your memory. When in dire need, give tongue to them and your enemies will flee. The words are in the Nyarlethu tongue. How does it happen that you can't read them?"

"I was raised as a thrall among humans, my lady. I can read only the common tongue . . . I know no other."

"Those words are great magic and were put there by a very great wizard to protect you. Uttered aloud, they will make the strongest enemies flee, so remember them well." A sweep of her palm erased them.

"I am grateful to you, my lady. I shall remember."

She seemed quite restored by the meal, and we set off up the path again to find a place to spend the night. When we came to the devil-flowers, she lifted up her hands, chanted a spell in an unknown tongue (unknown, at least, to me), and flames erupted from her fingertips and crisped the horrible things. It was upsetting to see them writhing like so many serpents as they died . . . was that a shrill, almost inaudible scream?

"Could you teach me that spell, my lady?" I asked.

"I could, but it would do you no good. To make it work takes powers and knowledge of arcane things that you don't possess. Sorry."

Upriver, we found an unoccupied cave which

looked safe enough. We carried great armloads of sweet grasses to spread for our beds. We stayed there three or four days, leaving only to forage for food at the edge of the forest. She kept treating my leg with the fruits, and by the time she was ready to leave, it was quite normal again.

At last, she decided to return to her own place and I became restless to continue my journey. At the parting of ways, she turned to me, saying, "Fare-you-well, warrior; may fortune smile on you."

I lifted my hand in salute. "I have a notion that we make our own fortune."

Her silvery laugh rang out. "How right you are."

She went her way and I never saw her more. The cave seemed distressingly empty without her, for she was my first real friend among the humans, except for little Rua so long ago. Why couldn't I get the girl out of my mind?

I waited until dark, ate the remnants of my dinner, then set out on my way upriver to my still-distant goal.

10

My horns were tingling . . . yet I saw no foe—
a tiny drug-tipped missile laid me low.
Then, in the burrows of the demon-men
I slew a godling and was free again.
                    —*The Song of Godranec*

As I pressed on northward, the cliffs on my right hand became lower, then vanished altogether, and the forest crowded close to the riverbank again. I was confident by this time and had no fear. There were always two or three moons in the sky, so I had no lack of light.

I was striding along freely, close to midnight, when my horns began to tingle. I paused and looked around. I moved my ax to the ready to repel enemies.

I saw nothing . . . but my horns tingled worse than ever.

Suddenly, a small dart a little over a hands-breadth long appeared in my arm. It seemed a child's toy, so I plucked it out and tossed it aside. It would take more than that to bring me down. Where in the name of Khanophet were they?

Then I started to get giddy and my legs refused to support me. I collapsed on the path. I was completely conscious but had no power to move. The accursed dart had been poisoned! Was I dying?

After a while, I decided in the negative, for I remained conscious but paralyzed. It was apparent that it was a drug of some sort but not a poison.

When it became apparent that I was unable to move, my enemies came out of hiding. They were hideous little people about a head shorter than I and not nearly so broad. They were completely hairless and their hides were a dirty white—not the healthy white of the Chalkhrondi, but a dead-corpse white, like that of slugs found under rocks, and they stank. Even their eyes seemed to have no color. They wore scraps of animal hide twisted about their loins. Some of it looked distressingly like human skin. Each of them carried a length of hollow reed and wore at his waist a leathern pouch containing darts such as the one they had used on me. They produced a crude stretcher, rolled me onto it, then a number of them grabbed the poles and they set off into the forest at a rapid pace.

Not far from the river we came to a hill that was too regular in form to be natural. In one side was a dark hole. I was borne into that hole by my captors.

I found myself carried through a tunnel that would have been just high enough to allow me to walk upright comfortably. It wasn't completely dark, for, once inside, I saw that there was a strange type of lichen growing on the walls which gave a cold green light, dim but sufficient.

As I was carried through the tunnels I saw caves, also lit by the strange moss, and more of the little people, including some females who were even more hideous than the males, if that were possible. We passed one cave where there was the smell of blood and a number of little men butchering a carcass—was it of a human? I shuddered inwardly. Would I wind up as their bill of fare?

Deeper and deeper into the earth we went, down a number of ramps and through seemingly endless tunnels, carved from earth, but the walls were hardened by a process that made them almost like rock. There was no wooden propping like humans build in their tunnels.

Finally we halted in a vaulted cavern where there was a rude type of altar with a dark hole in the floor behind it. Off to one side was a heap of weapons and clothing, obviously from previous victims. Then the thought struck me—victims . . . of what?

The little people seemed extremely apprehensive and looked with considerable fear on the dark hole behind the altar, a hole which appeared to run down vertically into the earth.

Rapidly they tied me to the altar. They tossed my weapons and my pack on the pile with the others, along with my ragged clothing, leaving me naked on the altar. Then one of them blew on a strange little horn . . . and they all fled precipitously.

I waited. Then I noticed that the drug, whatever it was that they had used on me, didn't quite have the effect they thought. The dosage hadn't been sufficient for a Nyarlethu and it was wearing off. Gratefully I felt the strength flood back into my limbs.

Then I heard a sort of scrabbling noise from the dark hole. I exerted my strength on my bonds—they gave, but didn't break. Then, from the corner of my eyes, I saw the monstrous head of a ghastly . . . something . . . protrude from the hole, and glowing red eyes regarded me hungrily. Fear lent strength to my muscles, and with a frantic heave, my bonds broke. I slipped off the altar and rolled away in a frenzy of activity as a multi-legged perversity of nature heaved itself out of the hole and reared above the altar where I had so recently been tied.

It was a centipede, but gods, how could it be so big? It's mouth, equipped with poison fangs, was large enough to swallow me whole. The thing stank, and at least thirty parthi of it was out of the hole; only Khanophet knew how much of it was still in the hole. I backed away, and stumbled against the pile of weapons. I tore my gaze away from my enemy and searched for my weapons where I saw the little men throw them. Ah—there they were. I snatched up my beautiful enchanted spear, and as the thing, with its fanged mouth wide open, lunged at me, I flung the spear at its open mouth, aiming to where its brain should be, if indeed it had one.

Apparently it did, for as I danced aside, using all my fabled speed to avoid the fanged mouth, it gave a hideous scream and began to pull itself back into the hole. I caught up my ax, which was lying nearby, and, dashing in, cut the head from the thing. I didn't want to lose my spear.

Streaming blood, the thing drew back into the hole in a reflex action. I waited until the head stopped moving, then retrieved my spear. I cleaned it on an old rag from the pile—then recognized my breeches.

With nothing more to fear from the monster, which the little people obviously worshipped as a god, I began to examine the heap of clothing and weapons, which had evidently belonged to other victims sacrificed to the monster. I found an almost new pair of breeches which fit me beautifully, and a good leather jerkin. What was this? a mail shirt? I caught it up and examined it. It consisted of a thin leather jerkin with overlapping scales of a strange metal which seemed to be stronger than steel, with a fraction of the weight. I had never seen its like before. I tried it on . . . it fit, though it was a little long in the arms and came almost to my knees. I hardly felt its weight. It should come in handy. I found a new pair of boots which fit me, and a dark green, heavy woolen cloak. Under the cloak was my own familiar pack with my rune-sword protruding over my left shoulder. I added a dagger to my armory, for I needed it in preparing my meat. I also discovered a steel helmet with a leathern lining and gorgets, which fit me. Thus clothed and armed, I felt I could face my little enemies again.

At the door of the chamber, I paused. How was I to find my way out of this place? Logic told me that if I went up every ramp I came to, that sooner or later I should come to the surface of the ground. It was sure that I couldn't stay here. I set off.

I hadn't gone far when I came to a ramp that slanted upward. I took it, but when I reached the top and rounded a bend in the tunnel, I came face to face with a half-dozen of the little men.

They saw the armor but were evidently ignorant of its use, thinking it as just another garment. Several darts struck me but bounced off the armor. They were surprised at this and it scared them to death. I didn't know if they realized that I had slain their god, but the fact that the darts now had no effect on me made them fear me in turn. I transfixed two of them with my spear and was among them, ax swinging, before they could move. I disposed of all of them except one who ran back down the corridor. I snatched my spear from the corpse where it had stuck and hurled it at the fleeing foe. It struck him between the shoulder blades . . . he dropped without a sound. I retrieved my spear, cleansed it as best I could on the rag of a clout the dead man was wearing, then continued my attempt to find a way out of these tunnels. They had carried me so deep into the earth that I expected to round a corridor and find Khanophet himself confronting me. From time to time I felt darts strike me between the shoulders, but I was wearing the mail shirt and they bounced off, or else stuck in my cloak. I paid no attention to them.

I continued to climb every ramp I encountered. I don't know how long I had been climbing, for time didn't seem to exist in this place. I came finally to a broadening of the way, a sort of half-cave. The tunnel continued on the other side. When I was about halfway across, the little men came boiling out of the larger cave in great masses, intending to haul me down through sheer weight of numbers. I saw a sort of alcove not far away where they had started to hew a side tunnel and had abandoned it. I put my back against that, so they couldn't get behind me, and faced them. They came with a rush. I planted my feet wide apart for leverage and swung my ax horizontally in a broad figure-eight and hewed them down by the dozen. My ax was moving so fast it was almost a blur. The battle was fought in dead silence, except for the sound of my ax hewing bodies and the panting of my adversaries. Their blood was green and it stank strangely. I fought on, tirelessly, stolidly, hewing them as if I were hewing wood for my supper fire. The corridor began to be choked with bodies, when a weird, squalling horn sounded and the survivors withdrew. It was evident from then on that they feared me, having never encountered anything quite like me. As a fully matured Nyarlethu, I was a little over five parthi tall, with the strength of a dozen humans. Compared to me they were as wicked little mechanical dolls.

The tunnel still slanted upward, which was a good sign. As I entered it again, I realized that my ax was not suitable for such close quarters, for I hadn't room to swing it. I therefore thrust it through the loops I had made in my pack to receive it, and drew my sword.

My sharp ears, swiveling backward, caught the sound of my enemies following me, but they evidently feared me too much to close with me again.

I turned into another tunnel slanting upward and, wonder of wonders, there was fresh air coming down it. This meant open air and freedom. I mended my pace, my boots finding easy purchase on the steeply slanting floor. I encountered guards, but I attacked them at once and cut them down. The beasts evidently had no way of communicating, and the guards had no idea of what had happened down in the tunnels until I came boiling out at them. All I chanced to meet in this place I hewed down without mercy.

Then, quickening my pace, I came to a broad place in the tunnel and on the other side, the brightly lit opening to the outer world. The pounding of little feet was coming closer, and I hastened across the open place and stood in the sunlit arch of the door and turned to look back. There, at the opening of the tunnel, were two or three dozen of the little demons, with more back farther in the tunnel. They had stopped and made no effort to come at me. Then it dawned on me that they feared the sunlight. I laughed at them and strode out into the blessed sunlight alive and safe.

I found myself on a broad ledge sloping upward. I followed it and found myself at the top of a cliff which ran east and west. Where was I?

My ears swiveled as they caught the sound of falling water . . . to the west? A waterfall! That meant that the river was that way. I strode rapidly westward, putting my sword away and drawing my ax as I went . . . I had plenty of room to wield it here.

I was alert for danger but I feared nothing from the little demon-men so long as the sun shone. I determined to put as much distance between me and their caves as possible before night fell again.

It wasn't long before I came on the river, which was roiling through a narrow opening between two huge boulders, fell about fifty times my own height to a pool where it lingered a while, then rambled on southeast on its long road to the sea. The noise of the waterfall was deafening, for there was a lot of water spilling over the cliff. How long had I been on the road now? I had lost count of the days. Oh well, it didn't matter. If I kept putting one foot ahead of the other and could fight better than my adversaries, I would eventually reach my goal.

I didn't want to be anywhere near the opening of the underground warrens when night came on, and, judging from the sun, it was a little before nooning. I therefore set off upriver as fast as my legs could carry me. I picked edible fruits which grew near the path and ate as I traveled but didn't waste time going into the forest to seek for them.

By nightfall I was bone weary, having had no sleep since the preceding day. I knew that I had put enough space between me and the demon-men that I was safe enough from them. I was wondering where I could lie up for the night and be safe . . . then I saw it.

It was a rocky hill that came close to the river's edge. About halfway up I saw the opening to the cave. Since my experience with the little demon-men, I was a little suspicious of caves. Keeping my ax at the ready, I investigated cautiously. It was a lovely cave, not deep, and there was a small opening in the roof of the cave at the back, which would make a good chimney. I shed my pack, then, going to the edge of the forest, I hewed a supply of wood which I piled up in my cave. I took my spear and, going upriver a little, took a huelgu, cleaned it, and bore the meat back to my cave. I barricaded my door with stones to keep the larger beasties out. Even the demon-men couldn't remove them without arousing me from slumber. I built a fire, roasted my meat, then rolled up in my blanket (which I had rescued along with my pack), and fell asleep. During my trek through the forest I had learned to sleep lightly. I got up several times to replenish the wood on my fire. A couple of times I heard something pawing at the stones which barricaded my door, but whatever it was soon wearied of the task and went away.

I decided to travel by day for a while. It was fortunate that I did, for I found no other cave as safe as the one I had just left, and soon after leaving it I saw some serpent-men trailing me through the forest, not too close, but keeping an eye on me. Their numbers increased. I kept my weapons handy.

I came to a place where the underbrush thinned and I saw that there were a considerable number of them gathered with obviously hostile intent.

I put my back against a large rock and unlimbered my ax to defend myself. Could I do it? There were so many of them! I was getting to the point where I actually enjoyed a good fight, so pulling me down wouldn't be easy and they would pay dearly for it.

11

One battle won, another circumvented,
I find peace for a while and am contented.
I, who had slain one narbo, find another—
the lizard-men accept me as their brother.
                              —*The Song of Godranec*

The serpent-people gathered in a tight band with obvious deadly intent. There was a breathless pause before the attack. Suddenly, a hissing cry came from somewhere in the rear and they melted back into the forest and I saw them no more.

I leaned on my ax, shoved my helmet back, and scratched my head in puzzlement. What in the name of Khanophet did that mean?

After a while, I shrugged my shoulders and resumed my journey. Very shortly I found out what it meant when, turning a bend in the trail, I encountered three creatures out of nightmare that I could only describe as "beast-men."

They were apelike in appearance but entirely

hairless. They resembled the snerg slightly except that they were three times as tall as I was and correspondingly broader. Their long, muscular arms touched the ground. They had no sexual organs at all and seemed, somehow, to be unfinished, as if they had been put together by a drunken sculptor.

I hadn't time to examine them too closely because they caught sight of me and charged. I could see that they had only rudimentary intelligence. I took care of the nearest by hurling my spear at him. The enchanted point entered his chest where the heart should be . . . if, indeed, he had one. He did. He seemed to come unglued and collapsed and moved no more.

I avoided the lunging grasp of the second by using my fabled speed. My ax hewed his arm off at the shoulder in the same motion.

I couldn't reach the head of the remaining beast because he was too tall. I retreated a little to draw him away from his wounded companion, who was bellowing and streaming blood. I let the thing charge me, ducked beneath his grasp, and hewed his leg from under him. As he fell, I hewed his head off. I turned to see where the other was and saw him dashing madly northward up the path as if Khanophet himself were after him.

I retrieved my spear, cleaned both weapons in the sand of the river bank, and followed my enemy.

I hadn't gone far when I saw a wave of strange lizards swimming shoreward, for my erstwhile enemy had bled into the water and the smell of blood had drawn the creatures. They weren't as large as the balhalim (true lizards) that had fought the scorpions farther south, but when I saw the open mouths of some of them, I knew they were deadly and probably poisonous.

Some of them attacked the corpses of the two beast-men I had left on the path, and farther up-river, more of the things were pulling down the beast-man whose arm I had hewn off. They evidently were attracted by blood, for their eyesight didn't appear to be very sharp and they never noticed me. I faded into the forest and fetched a broad compass to avoid the things, which didn't follow me. They evidently didn't care to get very far from the river.

Through the trees I could see a lake of considerable size which was probably full of the things. I avoided going near the place. At the north edge of the lake I came to a cliff which wasn't hard to scale. When I was on top I went to the river again, drank from its clear water, and pressed on, ever northward.

Soon I became aware that lizard-men were again trailing me through the edge of the forest. These were the same type of creature that had talked with me at my cabin in Gelsan. I knew them to be intelligent creatures and didn't fear them. What had the lizard-man said? "Not friends—not enemies either."

They showed no hostile intent but seemed only to be keeping me under surveillance.

As I traveled north, I noticed another strange thing. There seemed to be a dearth of beasts in the forest. I encountered no dangerous creatures of any kind and wondered why, for it wasn't natural. Even the omnipresent huelgi were missing, and I had to dine on fruits, and roots which I had learned how to dig by watching the snergs. At night I built and maintained a fire, but nothing bothered me and my nights were more peaceful than they had been since I left Gelsan. I got an idea and, taking a piece of metal from my pack, I fashioned a crude hook and, using some scraps of meat I had left from the last huelgu that I had killed and a piece of line, I managed to catch a couple of fish. I even managed to take some large ones with my spear. This was a welcome addition to the fruit diet, which was becoming monotonous.

About three days' journey after I had slain the beast-men, I came to a place where the trees came close to the river bank and overshadowed the trail. Suddenly, I rounded a bend in the trail and come upon a large number of lizard-people. They were watching something on the far side of them . . . something I couldn't see.

I approached cautiously. They sensed my approach and swiveled their necks to look at me. However, instead of attacking, they moved aside, leaving an opening through their ranks. I took it and they closed behind me. Then I saw what they had been watching.

It was another narbo web, almost invisible except where the slanting sunlight glinted off the strands. There, caught in the web, wailing in fright and watching the approach of a huge, hideous narbo, was a small Halzhengu child. I didn't know much about the life cycle of the Halzhengim, but it couldn't have been much more than a baby.

What should I do? I owed nothing to the Halzhengim. On the other hand, I was in their territory and they had made no move to attack me. Anyway, this was just a little baby, and by the fires of Khanophet, I wasn't going to let the narbo have it.

Dropping my ax as useless against a narbo, I took my spear and approached the little Halzhengu. It stopped wailing and watched, with its large, terrified eyes, as I approached.

I spoke soothing words to it, then, keeping an eye on the narbo, I began to cut the web strands with the point of my spear.

There was a murmur from the Halzhengim behind me as the strands parted. The spider, seeing its prey escaping, attacked me.

I had had experience with such creatures. I took the spear by its butt end and caught it between the eyes. The enchanted point pierced its brain and it threshed its life out, becoming entangled in its own web.

I watched it die and then, as it stopped moving, I retrieved my spear and finished cutting the little Halzhengu loose.

As the last strand parted, I took the little creature in my arms. It lay there, trembling but passive, as I examined it for injury. Not finding any, I set it on its feet. It raised its tiny tail for balance and scooted to one of the lizard-people whom I took to be its mother. She snatched it up and hugged it. Then she rubbed dirt on the strands which still adhered to the baby, after which she was able to pull them off.

I cleaned my spear by thrusting it into the ground a few times, then went over to pick up my ax. The largest of the Halzhengim approached me, his saurian face showing much nobility and the great muscles rippling under his scaly hide.

He lifted his right hand in the universal gesture of greeting. I repeated the gesture and waited.

"We talk?" he asked.

"If you like," I replied.

"We no understand," said the Halzhengu, speaking the common tongue with difficulty with a thick, hissing accent.

"You don't understand what?" I asked politely.

"We no understand why you free child. What is he to you?"

I shrugged. "Nothing, perhaps; but he was little and helpless and I wasn't about to let him be eaten by that thing." I indicated the dead narbo with a wave of my spear. "Why didn't you help him?"

"We no can break web of narbo . . . lose many people that way. Anything caught in web is doomed. We try ax, sword . . . nothing can cut. You cut web easy—why?"

I displayed the runes on my spear. "It's enchanted," I said. "It's the runes that did it."

A very old Halzhengu came up. There was the light of wisdom in his saurian face and he carried his right shoulder higher than his left and limped on his left foot. He examined the runes closely with his slightly rheumy eyes. "You wizard?" he asked in a quavering voice.

I grinned. "Not I. Those were put there by a wizard, but that was long before I got hold of it. Have you a sword?"

"Yes," said the chief. He said something in his own tongue and a young Halzhengu came up bearing a sword.

I approached the web with the chief and the old one, whom I took to be their shogan. I struck the web with the sword . . . it bounced off like trying to cut steel with a razor.

"Your sword doesn't cut the web," I said.

The chief nodded. "We know."

I took my spear and cut a couple of strands. "My spear does cut it."

"We saw."

I picked up my ax. "Now, I made this ax myself." I ran the edge of the ax along one of the web strands and it sliced through as readily as the spear had.

The chief asked, "You made ax?"

"I did."

"Ax cut web."

"It does."

"Why?"

I displayed the runes on the ax blade. "I put those runes on myself, copied from the spear."

I unslung my pack and rumaged around in it. I found the scribing tool I had brought from my cabin in Gelsan. Kneeling on the ground, with two very interested Halzhengim squatting beside me, watching my every move, I copied the runes from the spearhead onto the sword that the Halzhengim had given me. When I finished, I handed the sword to the chief. "Now try it on the web."

The chief swung the blade. It cut through the narbo web as easily as the spear had.

Solemnly he turned to me. "All time you in forest, we watch. We not friends, not enemies . . . just watch. We see you fight enemies and win. We like how you fight. Now all is changed. You rescue my son from narbo, and teach us how to save our people from narbo web. Now we friends, brothers. We no tell names up to now, for if enemy find name, he have power over you. Now we tell names. My name . . . Sthurr. I chief of tribe. This my kinsman Slaar . . . our krengu—magic man."

I smiled and bowed. "I am Godranec. I'm happy to be your friend, for I'll need all the friends I can get before I get out of this forest."

Sthurr bowed in return, looking strangely graceful as he did so. "We know where you come from and where you go. When you go north again, soon you come to city . . . no go into city."

"City? What city?"

"Very old city . . . dead city . . . forgotten city. Nobody live there except demon lords and beast-men. Death is least that can happen to you there. Dangerous for you near city in open, for beast-men find you and take you to city. You come home with us this night. You rest, then in morning we see you past city safe."

I thanked him and we went south again. I had new friends . . . but what of this dead city they talked about? Why was it so dangerous?

12

The lizard-men go back along the trail
and take me to a lovely hidden vale.
I teach my friends the art of forging; then,
upon the trail, destruction strikes again.
                                    —*The Song of Godranec*

For a couple of hours we went south to where I had
forded a small stream earlier. We went east along
the edge of the stream. There were many flowers
growing alongside the trail and no noxious beasts,
except that the trail curved several times to avoid
narbo webs. Many of these had Halzhengu skeletons
adhering to them. With enchanted weapons, I had
the idea that Sthurr would start a war against the
huge spiders.

In time we came to a high cliff, well concealed
by tall trees. In the cliff was a narrow opening some
ten paces wide. This passage curved, inside the
opening, so that it was all but invisible from a few
paces away. It looked as if it had been hacked out

of the rock by the ax of a giant. This narrow, crooked passage was guarded by Halzhengim with crude weapons. At the inner end, we entered a broad beautiful valley with a village in the center of it. The village swarmed with Halzhengim of all ages and sizes, who stopped what they were doing and stared at me. I must have looked strange to them. They had seen horned helmets before, but they had never seen a short, muscular creature with the horns on his head and not on his helmet.

"Not many people speak common tongue," said Sthurr. "I speak . . . Slaar speak, and one or two others. Common tongue comes hard with us."

"I can imagine," I said.

The largest house belonged to Sthurr, who took me inside and immediately set about making me feel at home.

There was a fireplace with a fire burning. There was a chair, old but comfortable, which he set for me, while he sat on a strange type of stool of a kind that I had never seen before.

"That chair belong to house," he said. "Have others but no use them, for we not built for human-type chairs."

"I see," I replied. "This village looks like a village of men to me."

"Was a village of men . . . long time ago," said Sthurr. "They no keep watch in passage . . . beast-men get in and kill all humans or carry them to forgotten city. We find village and dwell here. We can defend though we not have many weapons."

I found myself liking these beings who, in contrast to humans I had known, were gentle creatures who wanted nothing more than to be left alone.

The meal was quite normal—roast tharg, fruits, and some vegetables I could not identify but which were delicious.

I indicated the tharg. "Where did it come from? I have been concerned that there were no beasts in the forest near here, and I was getting tired of fish and fruit. Where'd you get the tharg?"

"You never notice," said Sthurr, "we have herd of them. Brought some with us from plains where we used to live. Much grass in valley, so thargs prosper. Beast-men kill all creatures outside the valley or carry them to dead city."

After we had eaten and were relaxing in the cool of the day on a bench by the door, I said, "You mentioned 'demon lords' who live in the forgotten city. Who are the demon lords?"

Sthurr shook his head. "Not know who. Not know where they come from. Shogan say they come long ago, slew people of city, and live there in palace. They make beast-men out of flesh of men and animals to be servants of them."

I frowned. "The demon lords *make* them?"

Sthurr nodded. "Beast-men no breed. Demon lords make them from flesh of men and captured beasts. They have many in city."

"It must take a lot of meat to feed them."

"Beast-men can eat, but not need to. Beast-men get out of city they eat anything they can catch . . . sometimes eat each other. No do that in city, for demon lords organize like soldiers."

"Why do the demon lords make so many of them?"

"Not know why . . . we no go there. Some of our people captured by beast-men and taken there . . . no see them again. We fear dead city worse than death, for what happen there, worse than death."

I pursued the subject further but got no more information, for evidently Sthurr didn't know any more. The main thing seemed to be that the Halzhengim seemed to have an inbred mortal fear of the dead city.

I had a bed that had formerly belonged to a human, a bed which proved quite comfortable. The next day I was, for the first time in my life, among friends. I went with Sthurr and a couple of his chiefs to explore the village.

One of the first things that caught my eye was a dilapidated building that had evidently once been a smithy. The roof was still sound and there were two forges which were still in good condition except that the hand-worked bellows were cracked and needed mending. There was even a good supply of charcoal and a quantity of iron and steel of various strengths, all waiting to be forged.

I turned to Sthurr. "You say you need weapons?"

"We do. What weapons we have we take from humans we kill. Formerly we live all over this land and no need weapons, for we no have enemies. We ate fruits, run down thargs, eat meat . . . eat things that grow wild. Was a good time.

"Then humans come . . . kill us on sight; drive us into forest where we live like beasts. Now, humans hate and fear forest. We afraid they get courage and come in with army and slay us. Need weapons to defend ourselves."

"You can make all the weapons you need right here."

"We know that . . . not know how to work machines."

"Maybe not . . . but I do."

"You can work machines?"

"I was a thrall in Gelsan and foreman of a larger place than this."

Sthurr asked eagerly, "You live among us and make weapons for us?"

"No . . . but I'll stay long enough to teach some of your people how to do it."

"Is good . . . start."

"There's one problem." I picked up a piece of iron which was slightly rusty. "We'll need lots of this."

"Is no problem. Cave in hills full of it. We just have to dig out of ground."

"Could you?"

"Easy. Up to now, no need to, for we have no use for it. Now you teach us to make weapons, we dig plenty."

I stayed with them for almost a month. I even found a smeltery in another building and taught the Halzhengim to turn iron into steel. As swords were made, Slaar, using my scribing tool, which I gave him, copied the magic runes onto them. Already the smiths were figuring out ways of altering the size and shape of the weapons so as to fit their own physique, and some of them were busily at work designing new weapons of a completely new kind. I prepared to resume my journey, knowing that my friends would be self-sufficient and able to protect themselves.

"You no stay longer?" asked Sthurr. "You our great and good friend. You save my son; you save our people by teaching us to make weapons. We want you stay longer."

"I'm afraid I can't," I replied. "My way is yet long and my own people are at the end of it. You are my brethren, but you can't imagine how I long for people around me of my own race."

He nodded. "We know. Not keep you. We no forget you."

"Nor will I forget you, my brother."

Sthurr and a number of strong warriors armed with the new weapons led me through the forest, avoiding the river until we were well beyond the dead city. I was a little curious about the city, but felt my friends were right and it would be well to avoid the place.

As we walked, Sthurr said. "I send word to others of our people to come, learn how to make weapons. We be safe from beasts who look like men, and from men who live like beasts. We have weapons better than theirs."

Well beyond the city, at the edge of the Volsek, I took leave of the first friends I had ever had in my two and twenty summers . . . except for little Rua.

Why couldn't I get the girl out of my mind? I was thinking deeply of her little pinched face and how she had died waving the bleeding stumps of her arms in the air and screaming for the help that never came. I never heeded the tingling of my horns until I caught a strange stink, and out of a dense thicket a swarm of about fifty beast-men came at me. I cast my spear at one and began to swing my ax in the blurring figure eight. There were too many for me, and they bore me down by weight of numbers. A club hit me on the back of the head and I knew no more.

13

A dismal cell greets my awakening sight,
the antique bars cannot resist my might.
I fight the beast-men, find a long lost drain,
and at its end, I find my friends again.
                                    —The Song of Godranec

I awoke slowly and painfully to find myself lying on
a pile of moldy rags breathing a dank, humid air
that hadn't much oxygen in it. I found myself getting used to it as I struggled back to consciousness.
My head ached but the pain grew less as I struggled
to my feet and began to walk around. I found myself in an underground cell of some sort, obviously
beneath the level of the river, for the walls were
damp and there were little puddles of water here
and there on the floor. The cell was a large one
with iron bars across the front of it, with a huge,
rusty antique-looking lock on the door. Where was
I? Obviously in the dead city, locked in a cell and
weaponless. Weaponless? No! By the fires of Khan-

ophet, I still had my sword strapped beneath my pack with its hilt over my left shoulder. Why hadn't my captors taken it away from me? The only reason I could think of was that the beast-men, being of very low intelligence, hadn't seen a sword before and didn't know what it was. I wasn't in darkness, for the cell was lit dimly, but adequately. Peering through the bars of my cell, I could see that there were strange devices built into the ceiling that shed a cold bluish light. Some were out and all showed great age. I had no desire to be here when they came for me, for it was obvious that I was only in a temporary holding cell until they—or someone—was ready to . . . well, I would rather not think of that. Could I break out? I began to examine my cell minutely.

The door was heavy and solid. No way out there. There was hope, for the bars, which had originally been strong and fixed solidly into the masonry, were now rusty and some were loose at the bottom.

I took off my pack and my cloak and lay down on the floor. I grasped one of the loose bars with both hands and braced my feet against its neighbor. Slowly I began to straighten out. The powerful muscles in my back bulged with the strain but . . . something was giving!

There was a grating noise as one of the bars came loose at the bottom and slowly bent towards me. I rested a little, then tried again. Eventually I bent the bars sufficiently to allow even my thickset body to pass. I shoved my pack and sword through the opening and followed. Once in the corridor, I donned my pack, picked up my sword, and, holding it naked in my hand, padded quickly to the door I saw at the farther end.

There was an antique lock on the door, but time had long ago rendered it inoperable. I found myself in a long, curving corridor. Cautiously I pursued it to see where it would lead.

I soon got into trouble, for one corridor opened into another in a veritable maze and I was soon lost. Grimly I kept going, for sooner or later I was bound to find a way out. I came to a ramp and ascended it, reasoning that I was underground and if I went up, I should certainly come to the surface eventually.

Rounding a corner, I came upon a couple of beast-men emerging from a room. They were surprised to see me, and before they could collect their dim wits, I attacked them fiercely and my enchanted sword cut them down.

From another room I heard screams of agony. Fortunately the door was closed. I fled past it like a shadow and didn't pause until I had put quite a distance and another ramp behind me.

I spied another door, open this time, and saw bins full of fruits culled from the jungle, and all sorts of edible roots. There was meat hanging from hooks on the wall, but, not knowing what sort of creature it had been taken from, I passed it up. I ate my fill of fruit, stuffed more in my pack, then resumed my quest for a way out of this place.

I found and mounted a couple more ramps with no opposition. In one corridor I came upon a small band of beast-men. The only thing that surprised me about that was that I hadn't encountered more of them. There were supposed to be a lot of them, but so far I had been lucky in avoiding them. I attacked and cut down some of them before they could react, and the others fled. Without doubt they would spread the word that I was loose. I had to find a way out, quickly.

The mazelike quality of the place got worse as I went along, and I hadn't the faintest idea of where I was.

I came to the top of a ramp and saw a large band of the creatures coming towards me with great clubs. I turned to retrace my steps and saw another band of them starting up the ramp. I fled down the corridor, turned a corner, and found myself in a cul-de-sac. I was trapped.

I backed against the wall to have something at my back so they couldn't get behind me. I felt metal. Turning, I saw a metal ladder fixed into the masonry of the wall. It was old but looked strong enough to hold *me*. It might collapse and kill me, but I should certainly die if I stayed where I was— die—or worse—for those screams still echoed in my mind.

Swiftly I sheathed my sword, then swarmed up

the ladder as fast as I could move. The beast-men came together at the foot of the ladder, in the place I had quitted only seconds before.

The ladder began to shake dangerously as one of the things began to climb up after me. I reached the top of the ladder and saw a low, narrow corridor. It was big enough for me but I doubted if the beast-men could negotiate it. That was good enough for me. I took it without hesitation.

The ladder collapsed a second after I quitted it, due to the weight of the beast-men trying to climb it. I grinned grimly at the bellows of pain from below. I was short and the tunnel was just large enough to allow me to walk upright. What sort of people had built it? There were a few of the blue lights here and there. How did those lamps make that light and how were they fueled? I longed to know but dared not stop to investigate.

The tunnel opened into a large tube which I recognized as a storm sewer. It was also lit at intervals with the blue lights. The sewer slanted and I reasoned that I couldn't be very far underground. Which way should I go?

If I went *up* the tube I would probably come out inside the city. However, if I went *down* the tube it was reasonable to suppose I would come out at the river, its only possible outlet. It was also reasonable to suppose that I would be free of beast-men, since they either didn't know of the sewers, or couldn't get into them—or both.

I went downhill, and after a journey of . . . I
don't know how long, for time didn't seem to exist
here, I saw a glimmer of daylight and felt fresh air.
My hopes were dashed when my way was blocked
by fallen masonry, which I could not dislodge. Farther back in the tunnel I saw a ladder leading upward through a shaft. It was a little more rusty than
the other, but it was try or stay where I was. Slowly
and cautiously, careful not to jar the ancient structure more than necessary, I began to climb.

As I climbed, I became aware of a tumult above
me and shouting . . . in what language? It sounded
like Halzhengim . . . but that was impossible. I
hesitated . . . then, as the ladder began to sway
dangerously, I decided I had to go up or perish.
Swiftly I climbed the last few parthi, pushed aside a
manhole cover, and grabbed the edge of the
masonry as the ladder collapsed beneath me.

I pulled myself out of the hole by the strength of
my arms. I was in a great square inside the city
near the wall, with the gate of the city not far away.
It had formerly been a market square, for ancient
booths were still in place with ancient moldered
merchandise still on the counters. I also found myself in the midst of . . . Halzhengim! By the fires of
Khanophet, there was Sthurr! He recognized me at
once and came over with an outstretched hand and
a wide grin splitting his ugly face.

"We come to city, try to free you," he said. "We
get into trouble. Look there."

He pointed to the other side of the square where a growing horde of beast-men were gathering, all armed with clubs and showing obvious deadly intent.

"We find your weapons," Sthurr said, handing me my ax and spear. "Not look like we can fight our way out of all those things."

"It doesn't look like it," I replied grimly, "but I'm happy to have these again."

I caressed my ax fondly. We had been through a lot together, my ax and me, and if we were to go, we would take a lot of those things with us. As I caressed the bright blade of it, I saw the runes that I had scratched into the blade with my scribing tool. When I saw the runes I had copied onto the blade from the sigil tattooed on my own flesh, the words of Mlada the spaewoman came back to me.

Speak them not but hold them in your memory, she had said as she wrote the words in the ground in the letters of the common tongue. *When you are in dire need, give tongue to them and your enemies will flee.* How had I forgotten this? Would it work?

If this wasn't a time of dire need, then I would never be in dire need.

I turned to Sthurr. "We aren't dead yet, my friend. I met a witch-woman in the forest who read me three words I have tattooed on my flesh. She said they were a strong spell and if I uttered them aloud, my enemies would flee. I'm going to try it . . . it can't do any harm."

"If you know spell," said Sthurr with conviction, "then use it. We need big magic to get out of this."

I stepped to the front and faced my enemies. Just as the host of beast-men began to lumber toward us, clubs upraised, I lifted my hands, and at the top of my great bass voice, I thundered out the three words that Mlada had taught me.

At once the light of the Vilarian double sun was obscured by a great black cloud that abruptly formed above us. From the cloud, a mighty, invisible force erupted with ravening power and literally bowled over the beast-men by the hundreds, mashing the nearest flat. A deep, sub-bass howling came from the cloud. The terrified creatures threw their clubs away and fled precipitously toward the half-ruined palace I saw in the distance . . . doubtless the tunnels where I had been confined lay under the palace.

With the square clean of our enemies, we made our way swiftly out the nearby gate. The massive halves of the gate were folded back against the outer walls, one of them hanging by one hinge. An arched stone bridge spanned the river. It was covered with bas-reliefs, to which scraps of color were still adhering. It was half ruined but still sound, so we went across it at the double-quick and soon lost ourselves in the forest.

When we were a safe distance from the city we stopped to rest. (Incidentally, I never could figure out what happened to the cloud after we left—I was too busy getting out of the accursed city.)

As we were resting, Sthurr said glumly: "We try rescue you, you end up rescuing us."

The look in my eyes left no doubt as to the love I felt for this great and gentle creature.

"It's the intent that counts, my brother," I said. "The very fact that you entered a place that you feared worse than death to rescue one who was alien to you and your people will be sung about by minstrels for centuries. I will see to it if I ever get to my own people again. It was bravely done."

"We no could let you be taken into city without trying to get you out," said Sthurr. "I would have gone by myself but these warriors wanted to go with me."

"It was well done," I said. "I thank you more than I can put in words."

He put his great hand on my shoulder. "We understand each other, brother. Say no more."

I went back to their village for a couple of days' rest. Then, when I started out again, a large band of Sthurr's warriors led by Sthurr himself went with me. We skirted the dead city by a wide margin, and my friends went with me two days' journey until we came to the edge of the forest. Then, after I said good-bye to my first real friends for the last time, they turned back into the forest and I continued into the grasslands alone.

14

An endless sea of grass absorbs my eye
to where the cloud-tipped mountains brush the sky.
The slayer slain, I take the road again
and come upon a band of little men.
                                    —The Song of Godranec

The sight of the great grassy plains was thrilling. There before me was zark after zark of waving grass, almost shoulder-high to me, as level as a floor that stretched all the way to the mountains, which seemed to be very close but which I knew to be day after day of weary march away.

I began to stride rapidly up the bank of the river, where the grass was not so high and I could get a better idea of what I was getting into. A brown-and-green tirilu soared into the sky, sending a cascade of silvery notes after it. All was peaceful. There were various grass-eating mammals not far away, going about their business. The sky was blue above and the river murmured peacefully on my left.

Suddenly, with absolutely no warning, a huge trapdoor banged open about a dozen paces in front of me and a hideous krongu, first cousin of the narbo, sprang out at me.

The spider was a dirty white and covered with stiff white hair, and stank. Its mandibles were large enough to snap me in two. I was saved only because of lightninglike reactions, honed by months in the wierwoods. I was carrying my spear in my right hand, ready for action, with the point toward the rear. It took only a fraction of a second for my arm to fly up and forward, almost as a reflex action. I hurled the spear and it sank for half its length between the great compound eyes. I flung myself wildly aside and narrowly avoided being run down by the thing. It still tried to get at me. I took my ax, which hung from my left hand by its retaining strap, and cut a couple of legs from under it, retreating out of its reach until the enchanted point of my spear did its work and the thing writhed in its death throes. When it stopped moving, I retrieved my weapon, cleansed it and the ax in the sand at the edge of the river, drank from the cool water, and resumed my march. I remained alert, for I never knew when one of the things would spring out at me.

It became evident that the lithikhari kept the great spiders' numbers down, for I saw no more for two days. Why weren't there more of them? Why weren't there more of the great wasps, for that matter? The only reason I could think of was that the number of spiders were kept down by the wasps. The wasps didn't multiply enough to become a danger because they would eat only the spiders, and so the two species kept each other in balance.

I was walking near the river a couple of days later when a krongu sprang from its nest and pulled down a full-grown tharg not fifty paces from me. It was dragging its kill to its nest when, with a great roar of gauzy wings, a huge lithikhar came from nowhere, stung the spider into insensibility, and carried it off. I went to the tharg, killed it with my ax to get it out of its misery, and carved off a haunch. I spent a couple of days in a little grove of trees by the river curing the meat over a slow fire so it wouldn't spoil (something I had learned how to do in Kula's kitchen). Then, with this store of food in my knapsack, I resumed my march.

A couple of days later I saw trees upriver. As I drew nearer I saw that I was approaching a forest of considerable size which stretched for a long way on both sides of the river. At this latitude, the Vilarian double sun was hot in the middle of the day, so the cool shade was welcome indeed.

I found edible fruits in the underbrush which added to my larder. I camped at the edge of the forest for a few days to rest. I managed to spear fish which proved delicious when grilled over a small fire. I noted with dismay that I would have to eat my meat without salt soon, for the considerable store of the substance that I had brought with me from Gelsan was almost gone and I knew no way of replenishing my supply.

The fish were easy to catch. I fileted some with my dagger, a weapon I had picked up in the burrows of the little demon-men, and smoked them over a slow fire. I added them to my pack.

A couple of days later I continued my way up-river beneath the canopy of trees. These trees didn't seem to have the menace of the trees of the wier-woods, and I was comfortable and quite at ease. I hadn't gone far before I realized suddenly that I wasn't alone. Eyes seemed to be watching my every move. My horns didn't tingle, however, so while I was wary and walked alertly, I wasn't too concerned.

After a half-day's journey, I came to the shores of a great triangular lake some ten zarks long and only the gods knew how wide, for it seemed to widen as it went north. It was obvious that I couldn't cross it, so I'd have to go around it.

I turned east along the shore of the lake, whose waters were tossing and sparkling in the sunlight.

Then my horns began to tingle, but only a little. Then I heard a high, crisp voice speaking to me in the common tongue with precise intonation as if it weren't native to the speaker.

"Hold, stranger. Move not. Drop your weapons."

I froze and dropped my spear. I loosened the retaining strap of my ax and let it drop also. Then I turned slowly.

There, at the edge of the trees, were a number of little men only about three parthi tall. They were swarthy of countenance, with black hair and well-kept black beards, clipped to a point. They were dressed in forest-green jerkins with trousers thrust into knee-length green boots. They had green hunting caps on their heads with soft pointed crowns, some of which were decorated with the feathers of wild birds of some sort. Each carried a short, heavy, double-curved bow which he gave every indication of knowing how to use. The nocked arrows were pointing at me, so I decided I would move carefully and not provoke them. Slowly and carefully I removed my dagger from its sheath with the tips of my middle finger and thumb and dropped it to the ground, where it stuck, quivering.

15

The little bowmen soon become my friends,
for goodwill racial difference transcends.
They welcome me into their wild domain,
and then conduct me on my way again.
                    —*The Song of Godranec*

The leader of the men regarded me sternly, something, strangely enough, that didn't seem the least
amusing in such a small creature.

"What do you do in the Forest of Addini, Nyarlethu?" he said.

"Is that what you call it? I am not acquainted
with this part of the country, for I have never been
here before."

"In the barbarous tongue of the Chalkhrondi,"
he said, "it is called *Haldo Stal Vren Zhingimo*, or
Forest of the Little Green Men. We call it the
Forest of Addini, and it is our home. What do you
do here?"

"I was a thrall to the Chalkhrondi at Gelsan," I

replied. "I escaped to freedom through the wier-woods. I was told that my people live at the source of the Volsek. The river vanished in this lake, and I was going around it so as to pick up the river again on the other side. I am here by chance and will be gone from your land again as soon as I may."

"You were a thrall of the Chalkhrondi?"

"Since babyhood."

"How came you there?"

"I don't know . . . I probably won't until I find my own people."

"You came through the wierwoods?"

"It was the only way I could avoid being recaptured."

"The wierwoods is a savage place."

"I saw nothing there that was more savage than the Chalkhrondi, who flay a man alive for wanting to be free."

The bows came down. "It is apparent," he said, "that you present no danger to us."

"I am no danger to anyone. I slay only to protect myself or to fill my belly. I take no pleasure in slaying . . . I'm not a Chalkhrondu."

"It is good. We have been watching you, but now you are near our village and we had to determine your intentions before permitting you to continue. Will you be our guest for a time?"

I grinned at him and raised my hand, palm outward, the universal sign of friendship. "It would be my pleasure. My name is Godranec."

He smiled and took my hand. "My name is Asshi Vrangimi," he said. "I am war chief of the Alua-thim people. Come; our village is not far."

I picked up my weapons and went with them, chatting pleasantly about the forest and the creatures living there.

Soon we came to a great clearing where there were a number of beautifully built cottages with thatched roofs and doorposts carved in fantastic shapes. It amused me, after a lifetime of being the only dwarf among a nation of tall humans, that in this village I was the tallest person there; for all the villagers were at least a head shorter than I and much more slender, though they were muscular for their size. Still, the cottages were large enough so I didn't feel cramped as I entered the one belonging to Vrangimi. He made me welcome and, when I removed it, he examined my mail shirt with intense interest.

"What is this garment?" he said, as he fingered the overlapping scales. "I've never seen its like."

"Nor have I," I replied, "until I was captured by the little demon-men." I paused. "At least that is what I call them . . . I never heard of them until they captured me."

"We've heard of them," Asshi said grimly. "Those who fall into their hands never see the light of day again."

"I almost didn't." I related to him how I had slain the god of the little demon-men. "When I was clothing myself," I continued, "I found this mail shirt, it fit me, so I appropriated it. It would be interesting to know where it came from. I know metal but I have never seen a metal as light and as strong as this."

I found that the Aluathim were really a gentle people who worshipped Ilaraneth, lord of Wyrd. They had a lovely little temple to him where they offered to him fruits and living flowers. The temple was full of built-in containers where flowering plants and trees were growing, for Ilaraneth's special instrument was life. He hated blood sacrifices, according to the priest in charge, and also hated those who performed blood sacrifices. I was naturally drawn to such a god and offered my prayers to him, along with the Aluathim. This raised me in their estimation.

Asshi Vrangimi and I got along famously. I stayed with him for almost a week. I met other villagers, including the chief, and we all became fast friends. I went hunting with them out on the grassland. They admired my prowess with the spear, and we brought back much game. I carried a large tharg home by myself. It would have taken a dozen of them to carry it.

"We have a problem," said Asshi, as we were dressing the meat.

"What problem?" I inquired as I disjointed the tharg with my ax.

"We can't eat all this meat, and it will spoil, and that will anger Ilaraneth, who doesn't like to see game killed unless there is a reason."

"Why don't you cure it?" I asked.

"Cure it? How?"

I showed them how to make a little hut and hang the meat in it; how to select sweet-tasting wood . . . a little green . . . and how to smoke the meat to keep it from spoiling—something else I learned the hard way in Kula's kitchen.

When I was ready to leave, Asshi Vrangimi and some of his men went with me to guide me on my road.

We skirted the edge of the lake for two days' journey. On the third day we came to another river, which Asshi called the Bokor. It came flowing peacefully in from the great grasslands in the east. It was fairly wide but not very deep. At the point where it emptied into the lake there were a number of great rocks thrusting up from the water, which made natural stepping stones where we could cross with ease.

We then emerged into the grasslands and bore westward, and after a couple of days' journey we came again to the Volsek, where I took leave of my friends. They returned to their forest and I resumed my interminable journey northward.

I found that this pleasant interlude in the forest renewed my vigor, and I strode northward with great joyousness.

I encountered serpents of various sizes, but it was no problem to avoid them . . . or to slay them. Nothing much happened until the second day of my march. It was early morning and just after breakfast. I hadn't been on the trail long when I heard a great roaring to the east and there, not three hundred paces away, a large, horned slith was fleeing for his life. Behind it came an argu zhladuo, the great bloodthirsty, carnivorous lizard some ten parthi tall, which ran with great speed on its powerful hind legs, balancing itself with its long tail. It was actually an immense, savage, and quite brainless distant relative of the Halzhengim of the wierwoods.

The great lizard caught the slith and slew it with a bite of its great jaws, then squatted down on its haunches to enjoy its meal.

It was not to be allowed to do this, however, for, from a clump of huge bushes not far away came another argu zhladuo. (The name means "demon of the plains" in Chalkhrondu.)

The newcomer attacked the first lizard, and there I was, crouched in the grass watching an epic battle between two of the most powerful and savage meat-eaters on the planet.

I was so entranced by the monumental battle before me that I forgot my own danger. I didn't come to realize it until the newcomer, being larger than its opponent, managed to get hold of its fellow reptile behind the head and bite its neck through—I could hear the bones snap. It stood on the corpse of its fallen companion and roared its triumph. Then the fickle breeze changed to the west and the thing winded me. It decided that a Nyarlethu would make a good dessert dish and came at me, mouth wide open, moving faster than I dreamed possible.

I had only time to hurl my spear at the open mouth, aiming at the small brain which would be there in the vicinity of the back of its mouth . . . and then I flung myself frantically to one side to avoid the slashing talons of the beast's forepaws. They ripped my back, though, but I was saved by my mail shirt. The force of the blow knocked me some distance away . . . I blacked out.

16

A rock-hard skull and my ensorceled spear
save my life again. I knew no fear:
I save an Aluathim girl from death
and rob Chalkhrondu raiders of their breath.
                              —The Song of Godranec

I came to my senses slowly. I sat up and looked around me. My enemy was lying not far away, with my beloved spear thrusting through his open mouth, quite dead.

I climbed to my feet, shook my head to clear it (lucky I had a thick skull), and, after bathing my face in the river, I felt as if I were almost alive again. My back was bruised but the mail shirt saved me from serious injury. I retrieved my spear, cleaned it in the sand of the river bank, and blessed the memory of the unknown wizard who had made the point which had saved my life so many times. After carving a good-sized steak from the dead slith for my dinner, to be eaten with salt and other condiments which I had received as a gift from the Aluathim, I made my way rapidly upriver, for the smell of blood was heavy in the air. It would draw predators, and I wanted to be as far away as possible before they arrived.

If there were many more argu zhladethi around I would be in trouble. As my luck would have it, there weren't. It stood to reason that their vicious habit of slaying each other on sight would keep down their numbers. I found out later that their numbers were also reduced by the fact that their females took no trouble to conceal their eggs and other creatures dined on them with great relish. I thanked Wok, the creator, that this was so, otherwise the whole plains would be overrun with the savage creatures.

Needless to say, I slept lightly and without a campfire, for a light would have drawn them from a great distance and I wasn't sure that they would fear fire. I was not troubled at night except by night insects, which were a pest.

One day I heard the roar of gauzy wings overhead and saw a lithikhar circling above me. I knew that they ate nothing but the giant spiders, so I kept still and watched.

I don't know how the wasp located its prey, but suddenly it dived to the ground about two hundred paces in front of me, pulled open a trapdoor by brute force, and dragged from the nest a large, struggling krongu, stung it into immobility, and bore it off. I trod warily in that region and kept to the sand of the river bank where possible. This held my speed down, but I was sure of not stepping on the trapdoor of a krongu.

Nothing more happened, and I saw nothing more dangerous than a few large serpents, which usually fled before me. Those that didn't fell prey to my enchanted spear.

After a few days, the river bent to the east and I saw a large forest of trees before me. Would there be more of the Aluathim there? It was most likely. I had a cloak of forest-green given me by my friend Asshi Vrangimi. This would help me in dealing with them, for the color and weave of the cloth were unique and it could only be had from the Aluathim.

Once more I felt eyes on me but my horns didn't tingle, so I strolled on, along the bank of the river, beneath the shade of the huge trees. I camped just within the forest and didn't hesitate to light a fire and cook some meat I had killed out on the plains. I was not molested during the night.

The next day I came to the banks of a long, crooked lake some four or five zarks wide at its widest and at least fifteen zarks long. I immediately christened it Long Lake.

I was following the shore of the lake, enjoying the beauty of the place, when shrill screams attracted my attention to the lake shore.

There, some fifty paces away, a small female of

the Aluathim was being carried toward the water by an immense crablike creature who held her in one of his huge claws. Why he didn't kill her I'll never know, for he was powerful enough to have clipped me in two with those immense pincers.

With the things I had encountered on my journey, I didn't fear this creature but regarded it as just one more obstacle to overcome. I bellowed loudly and ran at top speed toward it over the hard-packed sand.

It heard me, dropped its prey, and turned to meet me, waving its claws menacingly. I reasoned that whatever brain the thing had would be located at the spot where the eye-stalks joined its head, so when I was close enough I hurled my spear at that spot. The spear never missed. The chitinous covering of the thing was tough, but the ensorceled point of my spear hit exactly where I wanted it to hit and sank deeply into the thing's brain.

It still tried to grab me with its claws. My ax whistled through the air and clipped the claws off one by one. Then it tried to retreat to the water, but I hewed a few of its legs from under it, then watched impassively as it threshed on the sand, my spear doing its work.

When it stopped moving, I retrieved my spear in case another of the things would come out of the water. Then I turned to the woman, who lay where she had been dropped. Was she dead?

I felt her pulse . . . no, she had only fainted and

didn't look much the worse for her experience except where the giant claws had bruised her flesh but had failed to break her skin. I picked her up and carried her to the edge of the forest and laid her down in the shadow of the trees. She was very young, still almost a child, and was lovely, with the delicate beauty of her race.

I took my battered tin pan and fetched water from the lake and bathed her face. She opened her eyes and took a drink when I held the pan to her mouth.

"Thank you for saving me," she said in the common tongue. "Those things are fast, and we have never been able to slay one of them . . . their covering is too tough for our arrows. I thought I was dead, for sure."

"My spear is enchanted," I replied.

"We wondered about that," said a voice behind me. I kept my hands away from my weapons and turned to see a band of Aluathim looking at me with admiration in their eyes. One of them, a virile-looking little fellow, came forward and embraced the girl tenderly.

"Are you a wizard?" the leader asked.

"No. The spearpoint was enchanted long before I got hold of it."

"You are a great warrior to slay a thing like that."

"After what I encountered in my journey through the wierwoods," I said, "it wasn't hard."

While we were walking to their village farther up the lake, I told the story of my peregrinations in the wierwoods and we exchanged names. The girl, whose name was Zima, was the young daughter of the chief of the tribe and had just been married to the young man who was embracing her, one Arduo Zimethi, the war chief. I stayed with the tribe for almost two weeks and we became fast friends.

Naturally, I taught their shogan the secret of the runes, and he began copying them on the arrows of all the warriors of the tribe so they would penetrate anything.

"Our biggest problem," said the chief to me as we were lingering over our winecups one day, "is that the Chalkhrondi make raids on us for slaves, and our arrows aren't enough to overcome them. We have a small deposit of iron in the middle of the forest and we know the art of the forge but don't know how to make steel from iron."

"I do," I replied. "Usually it takes powered machinery to furnish enough air to burn the impurities from the iron. However, it might be possible to devise a bellows powerful enough to enable you to make a small quantity at a time."

I worked with their smiths and succeeded in devising a method of making steel from their store of iron, and taught their smiths how to make swords and axes. As the weapons were made, their shogan inscribed the runes of power on them and they ended up being very good weapons indeed. I became a great favorite of the little people.

The chief, whose name was Wok Branghini, presented me with a powerful war-bow and a large quiver of arrows. These people, as I have mentioned before, were highly skilled bowmen and had bows with double curves that were very powerful and very accurate. I practiced with my new weapon every day until I became a very good shot. It was beautifully balanced for my size and strength and none of the Aluathim could draw it.

I was preparing to leave when a scout came in, saying that a detachment of Chalkhrondi were approaching from the grasslands, mounted on zelphars.

At once warriors sprang to arms. I put on my mail shirt and picked up my weapons to join them.

"This is not your quarrel, my friend," said the chief. "Why should you put yourself in danger for us?"

"Because you have been kind to me and you are my friends," I replied. "Besides that, I was a slave of the Chalkhrondi for twenty years. Any time I can kill a few of them is time well spent. On to the battle."

We met the enemy in the shadow of the trees, where they couldn't bring their zelphars. They trusted, as usual, in their superior strength and size to beat down a people they regarded as weak and ineffective.

To their surprise, the Aluathim arrows cut through their armor like cheese. It would have been different, perhaps, if they had had bows, but the Chalkhrondi scorned the bow in battle and regarded it as a weapon only for hunters. So they were cut down by dozens of archers posted on the wings of the Aluathim force.

The rest of us, with the chief and me in the middle of the line, massed and met them with swords and spears, which I had taught them how to use. They covered themselves with round shields which I had taught them how to make, fighting in close order using spears and swords as thrusting weapons.

I had no shield but fought in advance of the line, my bright ax whistling in a great figure-eight, each swing cutting down at least two of the enemy. They were astonished to see this stocky Nyarlethu in such a place. Even as they were stronger than the Aluathim, so I was as powerful as any ten of them put together, and my ax seldom sang in vain. Soon I was standing on a heap of enemy corpses, hewing heads and bellowing lustily at the top of my lungs with pure joy of battle. The Aluathim were by no means idle. Finally, seeing they couldn't win and were like to lose all their lives, our enemies broke and fled for their zelphars. They vanished into the grasslands as fast as their mounts could carry them, and it would probably be many a day before they dared to come back to this place.

I lingered among my friends for a few more days. Then, with a supply of smoked meat, salt, and other condiments in my pack and my new bow on my shoulder, I said good-bye and resumed my weary trek northward.

17

I fight my way into the rolling hills;
the nearby mountains shake my soul with thrills.
I slay some wolves, and get some breathing space,
then, suddenly, I see a strange, wild face.
                                    —*The Song of Godranec*

I saw a few lithikhari, but, as usual, they didn't pay any attention to me. I also saw a couple of argu zhladethi, but they were some distance off, and with a green turban wound about my helmet and the green cloak, gift of the little people, and only my head showing above the grass, the killer lizards didn't see me.

I began to see some skaldu birds far above me. They were huge birds of prey, powerful enough to carry off a full-grown slith. They needed a lot of meat to survive, so even if they did see me in my green cloak, it was highly doubtful that they would attack me when the plains were swarming with thargs and sliths for the taking.

THE ALIEN

The first sign of trouble came the third day out when an immense, green, many-legged worm came boiling out of a hole in the ground and attacked me.

I found the limitations of the bow, because I didn't have time to get it off my shoulder, much less to string it. However, as usual, I had my trusty spear ready and flung it by reflex action. The enchanted point went into the wide-open mouth of the thing and buried itself in the brain. It went into convulsions and bled a thick, greenish blood which stank.

I watched my chance and danced in swiftly, severing the head of the creature with my ax. The thing had almost stopped moving when I retrieved my spear and retired to a safe distance, or so I thought. A second one of the creatures erupted from another hole to see what the odor was about. Fortunately, the things were cannibalistic, and while the newcomer was dining on its unfortunate neighbor I was able to slip up and pin it to the ground with my spear. I slew it like I did the first one. Once more I blessed the memory of the unknown wizard who had made the point that had been my salvation so many times. I cleaned my spear, then, keeping close to the river and walking on the sand, I managed to get by the place without attracting any more of the things. I don't know how many lived there or even what their names were, or if indeed they had names, since it was probable that anybody who attracted their attention would not live to tell about it. I survived only because of my speed and my enchanted spear.

As I resumed my trek northward the mountains drew closer and closer and somehow they thrilled my very soul. I had a strange sense of coming home . . . though, to my recollection, I had never been there before.

I saw lithikhari incessantly hunting the great spiders and finding them. I never encountered krongus close to the river here, I don't know why, unless it was because the ground was sandier here and there would be water seepage in their burrows. Whatever the reason, they dug farther out on the prairie, which spared me the danger of stepping on one of their burrows.

I did find a few giant scorpions, but they weren't as large as those of the wierwoods and didn't run in packs, and it wasn't difficult to take care of them with my spear, which, according to the spell of the wizard, never missed. It didn't harm me, though, so I must have been pure at heart. (I wonder what that means?)

One day I rounded a bend in the river where there was a huge outcropping of rock that I had to go around. When the river came in sight again I saw an immense wolf drinking from the river. From the Aluathim I knew that the things ran in packs, but this one was alone, which meant either that it was an outlaw or too old to run with the pack.

THE ALIEN

He saw me as soon as I saw him, and attacked me at once. The thing could move almost as fast as I could. I had only time to hurl my spear at his heart before I flung myself aside to avoid his gaping, slavering, stinking jaws.

The spear flew true . . . but the beast didn't fall. Instead he whirled and attacked me again, moving a little slower this time due to the wound.

I stood my ground, and when he was close, I buried my ax in his skull. He shook his head and I was flung some distance away.

I retained my hold on the ax because it was fastened to my left wrist by the retaining strap. I was stunned by the fall. When I clambered to my feet the beast, with his head split open, was lying some twenty parthi away, kicking his last. He was as tall as my shoulder and powerfully built. I felt proud that I could slay an animal like that without being slain in return. I extracted my spear with some difficulty, then resumed my journey.

Soon the ground began to rise into the foothills which bordered on the mountains. Here the grass was shorter and there were bushes and trees which could conceal enemies, animal and human. I walked warily, keeping on the alert and always keeping my weapons at the ready. The spear, which had saved my life dozens of times, was always in my right hand, butt foremost and spearpoint to the rear, ready for my arm to fly up and back, then sweep forward to hurl it.

I hadn't had need for my bow yet except to kill some game to fill my belly. For real danger, it was not in the class with my spear, for it took time to string it and I could be dead by that time.

The sun was far westering when I sought a place to spend the night. I had a large canteen, a gift from my Aluathim friends, who had taken it from a human they had slain. I saw a large rock near the river with difficult access, but it could be climbed. I filled my canteen from the river, after drinking my fill. Then, gathering a supply of dry sticks for my evening fire, I climbed to the top of the flat rock, which was more than twenty parthi high, and built my fire and began to cook my supper.

I soon became aware that I had company, company who had also come for supper—namely for me. I peered over the edge of the rock and saw about twenty great wolves sitting in a circle all around the rock, looking up at me with great scarlet eyes. They were perhaps the companions of the wolf I had slain and had evidently followed my trail after finding their dead fellow.

Oh, well, I was safe enough for now. It was evident that they couldn't climb the rock or jump that far for all their size and strength. Maybe they'd get discouraged and go away.

I ate supper, watched the sun set over the desert to the west, then rolled up in my battered blanket and went to sleep. I still slept lightly and had learned not to toss about and roll, so morning found me quite refreshed.

I ate the remains of my supper and drank the last of my water . . . then remembered my guests.

I looked over the edge of the rock . . . and they were still there, sitting in a circle, watching silently with their great red eyes. It was apparent that they were waiting until I should get thirsty enough to come down. What could I do?

Ah! The great bow the Aluathim had given me. It should come in handy now. I examined my quiver . . . there were plenty of arrows. It was sure that I didn't want to face so many of the beasts with spear and ax.

I strung my bow, selected an arrow, and examined my enemies with a critical eye.

That largest one over there was evidently their leader. How about him? I nocked the arrow, a hunting arrow longer than my arm, with runes scratched on the steel arrowhead by the Aluathim wizard.

I noted the direction of the wind, allowed for it, drew the arrow to my cheek, sighted carefully, then let fly.

The bow twanged lustily and the arrow appeared abruptly in the heart of the beast. The things were hard to kill though, and had a lot of life, for the thing roared and threshed around for quite a long time before it succumbed. The others circled about nervously, then finally stopped, sat down again, and watched me.

One by one I slew them until all were lying still with my arrows in them. When they stopped moving, I clambered down from the rock, and with my ax ready, I went about collecting my arrows.

The last one wasn't quite dead, but started up as I tugged at the arrow. I beheaded him with a blow of my ax, and cleaned my arrows quickly in the sand of the river. Then, filling my canteen swiftly, I made my way upstream as fast as I could go, for the smell of blood was sure to draw any predators in the vicinity.

As I worked my way farther into the foothills the country became ever more wildly beautiful. I encountered no serious predators, for the most dangerous of these were probably on the plains where the game was. I saw a few bears, but they kept their distance, and I was happy to let them do so, for they were dangerous when aroused. There were a lot of small predators that preyed on small rodents. My sharp eyes saw them slinking among the rocks but they presented no serious difficulty.

So it was with intense surprise that I arose from drinking at the river to see a strange, wild face glaring at me from a clump of bushes.

18

The mountains! I could feel my spirits soar.
The hills of home! Had I been here before?
The stream I follow through the mountain's core—
my final foe attacks me with a roar.
                    —The Song of Godranec

It was a face not unlike my own, but strangely different. It had pointed ears, but the eyes were a pale color . . . (blue? grey?) and not slanted as mine were. The hair and beard were long, almost to the waist, and the light of madness was in his eyes. The sex was easy to determine because he was quite naked. It was almost as if he were a cross between human and Nyarlethu . . . but that was impossible—wasn't it?

Suddenly, as if a light winked out, he was gone. I went to the clump of bushes and saw nothing. It was as if the earth had swallowed him. Who and what was he? I burned to know but knew that search would be in vain, so I put it out of my mind and continued my journey.

Day by day I mounted through the foothills, the river ascending on my left in a series of rapids and falls. One day I encountered a sort of road coming in from the desert to the west, fording the river, then curving north along the east bank of the river. Who had made the road and what sort of beings were they?

I was grateful to the road, for it helped me make good time, and the way was better underfoot.

In a couple of days the foothills disappeared and I entered a long, broad valley which was more beautiful than I had ever seen before. The river meandered gently through the middle of it with lovely trees on either side, some of them fruit trees of various sorts. I reveled in the fruits for I was a sort of fruit-o-maniac and hadn't been able to get enough of it since leaving the wierwoods.

There was a burst of bitter resentment when I spotted a group of a dozen humans camping up ahead, scattering refuse around, as they always do. They had apparently been hunting, for they had some small deer and a couple of medium-sized cats. Their zelphars were tethered not far away, cropping the lush grass.

The humans saw me as soon as I saw them, and they seized their weapons and came at me, evidently intending to take me as a thrall.

I had had quite enough thralldom of the humans,

so I put a rock outcropping at my back so they couldn't get behind me, and I unlimbered my ax. They had left their lances behind, for they could only be used from the backs of zelphars, and were armed with nothing but swords. They had bows, of course, but never used them because they wanted to take me as a thrall. They trusted to their numbers to overcome me.

They had no idea of how fast I could move. Also, I had been living in the wild for over a year and my muscles, much more massive than those of the humans, were as hard as stone. I discovered later that while humans matured between fifteen and twenty-two, a Nyarlethu didn't attain his full growth before the age of thirty. Therefore, my strenuous life in the wild came just as my body was maturing, and I was much more powerful now than when I had left Gelsan.

My ax promptly sliced the belly out of two of them. The survivors threw themselves on me, intending to bear me down by weight of numbers. I freed myself by standing with my powerful legs wide apart and shaking myself like a bear. The humans were unable to hold on and flew off in all directions. This made them angry and they abandoned any idea of taking me alive. They drew their swords and attacked me. My ax swung in its shining bloody double circle so fast that their eyes could hardly follow it. In an astonishingly short time all except two lay dead or dying. Those two took to their heels and ran toward the cover of the trees. I snatched up my spear and hurled it at one, transfixing him in the center of the back where the point sank into his heart . . . he moved no more. Snatching up my bow, I quickly strung it and put an arrow into the neck of the last one just as he gained the cover of the trees.

Cleansing my weapons, I went through their baggage. They had little I could use, except dried fruits, salt, and other condiments, some of which I hadn't seen since leaving Gelsan. Naturally anything I could use went into my pack.

The zelphars were pawing restlessly because of the smell of blood. I had no need of a zelphar. I spoke gently to them in Chalkhrondu, and after calming them, I removed their saddles and bridles and turned them loose. They took off at once towards the prairie.

The brief but frenzied battle made me thirsty. I drank from the river, then finished off a bottle of wine I found in the baggage of the humans, then resumed my journey upstream.

I was entranced by the beauty of the valley. The trees quite often bore flowers, and the wild loveliness of the place left me breathless.

I didn't hurry here, for the place was so fantastically beautiful that I had the idea I was home already. I just enjoyed myself. I walked on until I encountered something that seemed to demand my attention. Then I would sit down in a convenient place and look my fill. When I was sleepy I would lie down in the sun, or in the shade of a tree . . . as my whim dictated . . . and take a nap. After what I had been through this was paradise.

I kept seeing bears, but, though the beasts were large, they tended to their business and I tended to mine. I hoped I would not encounter cave bears, which were huge beasts extremely irascible and mean and would attack anything on sight. They were as black as Khanophet himself, while the bears I kept seeing were smaller and brown in color. So long as I could keep away from females with cubs, I was safe enough.

After about a week and a half of leisurely travel during which time I saw nothing more dangerous than the bears and a few small thunder lizards (about five handsbreadths tall and no danger to me), I came to a lake at the head of the valley. The river continued on the other side of the lake, where it vanished in a large tunnel.

It was evident that the valley where I found myself, lovely as it was, was not the source of the river, for the stream went into the mountain. Therefore, in order to find its source, I would have to follow it into the tunnel.

My resolution to do so was strengthened by the fact that the road I was following went into the mountain itself. I followed the road around the lake to where the water came gushing from the cliff. I saw that the river had cut the tunnel originally, but that the opening had been artificially enlarged, for I could see tool marks on the wall. It was now wide and tall enough to admit some very large beasts of burden, for I could see their droppings on the tunnel floor. The way wasn't entirely dark, for some of the luminous lichens had found their way inside and furnished enough light for me to see where I was going. I gripped my weapons at the ready in case I should encounter any cave bears, and moved boldly into the semi-darkness.

The lack of light bothered me a little. It wasn't dark, but it wasn't light either. I almost lost my way a couple of times when side tunnels branched out from the main one. The side tunnels were smaller and I reasoned that the people who had brought the beasts of burden in here were the people I sought, so I followed the droppings. There was confusion in the fact that the tunnel didn't always follow the river. However, I always picked the river up again, so it was never far away, and I could hear it when I couldn't see it.

Finally, I caught a glimmer of daylight ahead and the feel of fresh wind on my face. I mended my pace and the glimmer of light grew to an immense archway cut from the living rock of the mountain. There was a large level place just inside the door, and I broke into a run, eager to be out in the sunlight again.

I was halfway across the open spot when, with

an earthshaking roar, an immense cave bear came charging out of a side tunnel at me.

Swift as thought I hurled my spear. It struck the beast in the chest and sank into the place where his heart should be if he had one. This was by no means certain, for the enchanted point failed for the first time and the beast didn't seem to be greatly discommoded by the weapon. A swipe of his great paw broke off the shaft and left the point imbedded deep in its body. He came at me again.

I took a double-handed grip on my ax. I slipped aside, narrowly avoiding a huge-clawed paw, and took a cut at the great beast's head.

I missed the head and opened a long slash behind the left ear. This only infuriated the bear, who rushed madly at me, jaws agape, and narrowly missed me. He went far enough beyond me to enable me to shake off my pack and cloak, for greater mobility, before he came at me again.

This time the bear anticipated the ax blow, caught it with a great paw, broke the restraining strap, and sent the ax spinning across the cave where it splintered against the wall.

The beast reared up on his hind legs, intending to fall on me and crush me with his weight. I had only one weapon left.

I reached over my left shoulder and whipped out my sword. I held the weapon in both hands high above my head. As the bear came down the sword penetrated his heart. Roaring with pain, he heaved

179

himself up away from the devil-object, tearing the sword out of my hand. A blow of his paw caught me on the side, I felt myself flying through the air, out into the sunlight, there was a bone-splintering impact, and I knew no more.

19

I wake up in a wondrous, strange new place;
I meet a lovely girl—of my own race!
I find I'm heir apparent to a throne . . .
the alien is now no more alone!
                    —*The Song of Godranec*

I awoke in a soft bed with an anxious face bending above me. As my vision cleared, my heart gave a mighty leap into my throat, for the face was young . . . and lovely . . . and—wonder of wonders— that of a girl *of my own race!* Her large slanted golden eyes with the slitted pupils were full of concern. She had long brown-gold hair hanging down her back in braids and the cutest pink horns. She was a little shorter than I but intensely femi- nine, with ripe lush curves . . . all in the right places. Suddenly, magically, I was in love for the first time in my life.

She read it in my eyes and blushed slightly. She

said something in a tongue that I couldn't understand.

Seeing the blankness in my eyes, she switched to the common tongue. "You don't understand Nyarlethu?" she asked in a musical soprano.

"No, my lady, I speak only the common tongue . . . and Chalkhrondu."

"How do you feel now?"

"As if I had been eaten by a thunder lizard. My head aches but it's clear. I'm hard to kill, and after what I've been through getting here, a cave bear is only just another wild animal. Where am I?"

"In the halls of Dwornghee in the mountains of the Nyarlethim. I am Dweena . . . this is Dworn, my father, the king of Dwornghee." A noble-faced Nyarlethu appeared and smiled.

"No doubt you have a strange story to tell, my son," he said in a pleasant bass voice.

"Strange enough, my lord," I replied. "Who is that noble lady I see there?"

"That is the Princess Narda, my sister," said the king. "Pray tell us your name."

I shook my head to clear it, for the Princess Narda was the face that I had always seen in my dreams, older now, but lovely and somehow tragic.

"My name is Godranec, my lord."

"Godranec!" The Princess Narda caught her breath.

"Whence came you, young man?" asked the king, his eyes strangely eager.

"From Gelsan, my lord. I escaped thralldom there and made my way northward, for I heard that my people dwelt at the source of the Volsek."

"Who kept you in thrall?"

"A Chalkhrondu by the name of Bdengi. He had a large smeltery. Just before escaping I was foreman of the plant."

"Escaping the Chalkhrondi was a great deed, my son," said the king. "Few ever escape their clutches."

"I know it well. I was forced to watch as an escaped slave was flayed alive for trying to be free. I got away by going through the wierwoods where humans fear to travel."

Dweena's soft eyes widened. "You came through that awful place?"

"It was the only way, my lady, unless I wanted to stay a thrall all my life, or until Bdengi got angry with me and slit my throat, as he did one thrall who angered him. At least in the wierwoods my survival depended on nobody but myself."

"How long were you a thrall of the Chalkhrondi?" asked the Princess Narda.

"Bdengi said he found me walking down the road outside of Gelsan when I was only a baby, my lady. I couldn't have been more than two at the time. I'm two and twenty now."

"You must have had many adventures in the wierwoods," said Dweena.

"I did. Not counting the beasts I had to slay, I

183

was captured by the little demon-men who dwell in burrows and tried to sacrifice me to their god, an immense worm. I slew it and escaped. I was captured by beast-men and taken to the forgotten city and . . . well, it would take too long to tell it now. Someday I'll relate the whole tale."

I winced as I tried to move my left arm. I found it in a splint and wrapped in a thoroughly professional manner.

"You have a broken arm and a couple of broken ribs," said the king.

"Oh, yes, that blasted cave bear. It struck me just as I thrust my sword into it. It knocked me flying . . . I don't know where I wound up."

"Dweena found you outside the cave. The bear must have knocked you completely out of the door. If you hadn't been wearing that helmet and that mail shirt, you'd probably have been dead. Where'd you get that mail shirt? I've never seen metal like that."

"Nor have I, my lord. After I slew the god of the little demon-men I found it lying on a pile of gear and clothing, stuff that had belonged to former victims. It fit me and I took it."

"There was a sword sticking in the carcass of the bear," said the king, "a sword that had runes scratched on it. There was also a broken ax against the wall with the same runes."

"Yes, my lord, and there is a spearpoint still in the bear with the same runes. The spearpoint was made by a wizard. The other runes were copied from the spearpoint. By the way, I want that spear back . . . it saved my life a dozen times."

"You shall have it . . . my men will find it when they skin the carcass out. Killing that bear was a great deed, my son. It has kept us bottled up in this valley for months. We haven't been able to slay it and have lost many men trying."

"I had enchanted weapons. When it attacked me it was him or me—I preferred it to be him."

The king smiled. "I wanted to talk to you about those weapons. Where'd you get that ax?"

"I made it, my lord. I am a skilled worker in metals."

"The runes of power you have accounted for," said the king. "We are particularly interested in that other device on the ax . . . the crescent with the initials . . ."

"Oh, that . . . that signifies ownership to me."

"Oh? How so?"

"I bear that mark on my own breast."

"Show us," commanded the king, his eyes shining.

I dropped the coverlets with my good arm, pulled my shirt aside, and displayed the logo tattooed on my breast.

King Dworn and the Princess Narda bent over the logo, then looked at each other in wonder.

"Can it be he?" whispered the princess with tears in her voice.

"It has to be, sister," said the king. "I know the work of my brother, the wizard Groll, and I saw him put that logo there with my own eyes. There can't be two such marks."

He turned to me. "How long have you had that mark there, Godranec?"

"It has always been there, my lord. A spaewoman I met in the forest told me it was a potent spell to protect me from my enemies. She taught me the spell by writing it on the ground in the runes of the common tongue. I used it against the beast-men in the forgotten city and it knocked them over like a giant ax." I looked at them in wonder. "What does this mean? Why do you look at me like that?"

The king's voice grew tender.

"Know you, Godranec: Over twenty years ago, my sister had a son whose name was Godranec. My brother Groll, who is our wizard, put that logo on the child's breast as part of the birthing ceremony. All male children of our family bear it . . . I bear it on my own breast." He pulled his robe aside and displayed the twin of the logo on his own breast, except for the initials. "The 'S. N.' on your logo stands for *Shoga Nougan*—son of Nougan in the common tongue. Nougan was the child's father . . . he was lost in a mysterious cave-in.

"The child was two when his mother took him out into the valley to play. A great bird swooped down and bore the child off. We discovered later that the bird was Krugh, a half-human renegade who was then apprenticed to Groll and who had learned the spell for shape-changing. When he returned, Groll trapped him, took away his mind, and banished him, for it was he who had slain Nougan and plotted to take the throne of Dwornghee for himself."

"I saw such an one," I said.

"Where?" asked the king.

"In the valley outside, when I first came into the foothills. He was a little taller than I . . . slender . . . had light blue or grey eyes. He had pointed ears, but his eyes were human and there was the light of madness in them."

The king nodded grimly. "That was Krugh. He should have been dead by now. When Groll returns to Dwornghee, he shall learn that Krugh still lives.

"At any rate, you come here with a strange tale of being found outside Gelsan when a child—who would be the same age as my nephew. You make weapons and wend your way through dangers which would have killed an ordinary being and drop down on our doorstep with that logo still on your breast. There could not be two such marks. Sister's son, you have journeyed far . . . but welcome home."

I listened to the recital with growing wonder and excitement. "Home? You are my uncle?"

He put his hand on my head. "There is no doubt. I am."

". . . And this is my mother?"

Narda dropped to her knees beside the bed and embraced me tenderly. "I am your mother, my son . . . there can be no doubt, for in you, my husband Nougan lives again."

As the full import of their words struck me, my own eyes filled with tears.

"Yes," I said dreamily, "there has always been a dream in the back of my mind . . . a dream of a flowering valley with a big lake in the center and a gentle, loving face . . . a face of my own kind . . . your face."

"It wasn't a dream, my son," she said. "It was a memory." She kissed me tenderly.

"I have always been alone," I said, as if to myself. "I was Godranec the alien . . . Godranec the misshapen and the ugly . . . always alone . . . never more than merely tolerated. Even Bdengi was kind to me only because I was valuable to him. The only human who ever liked me was a little girl thrall I met when I was only a boy . . . and the overseer butchered her soon afterward."

"They slew her?" asked the king.

"The cook chopped her hands off because she broke a dish . . . then she let the girl bleed to death."

"Did they do anything to the cook?" asked the king.

"Certainly not," I said grimly, "but I did. Just before I left Gelsan I went to the cook's room and cut her throat and exulted as she died. The only beings who ever loved me were the Halzhengim and the Aluathim."

"The Halzhengim?" asked the king. "The lizard-people? I thought they were only a legend."

"No, they're real. They are really gentle creatures and extremely intelligent. I taught them how to make weapons to defend themselves. Compared to the Halzhengim, humans are only wild beasts."

"Who are the Aluathim?" asked Dweena.

"A little people who live in the forests along the river on this side of the wierwoods. They are shorter than we and much more slender. They are marvelous bowmen." I saw my bow standing in the corner. "I received that bow of them as a gift."

I paused, then continued. "I always have been alien and alone," I said. "It'll take time for me to get used to having people of my own, a family, a mother . . . and uncle . . . and . . ." I broke off.

Dweena grinned. "And a wife."

I stared at her. "A wife?"

"If you'll have me." She put her soft warm hand on my forehead.

"But if I am the son of the Princess Narda, and you are the daughter of the king," I said, "that makes us cousins. May cousins marry?" I asked the king.

He nodded and grinned back at me. "Among our people, cousins may marry. What says my nephew to the idea of having a wife?"

I grinned wider. "I like it well . . . very well indeed."

"Know you, Godranec," said Dweena gently. "Humans would regard you as misshapen and ugly, for you are not as they are. We do not regard you as such. To me, you are handsome indeed, and I have never seen a Nyarlethu as powerfully built as you are . . . and your muscles are as hard as stone."

I caressed her with my good hand. "If I hadn't been powerfully built and lightning-quick on my feet, I should have died a hundred times."

"Well, my dear," she said softly, "you are alien no longer. You are home with your own people and there will be great rejoicing in Dwornghee."

Her sweet mouth came down on mine and she did something with her tongue that was completely new to me and which made the sparks fly from my horns and caused my blood to boil.

She broke the caress all too soon. "Now," she said officiously, "my husband needs quiet so he can get well. Let us leave so he can get some sleep."

Later she came back with some nourishing soup, which she fed me with her own hands. She also changed the dressings on my wounds. I slept and received visits from my mother and the king. There were visits from Groll, a noble-faced old Nyarlethu with the wisdom of ages on his timeless face. He had been away from the Ghee on business, business which none dared question him about. He greeted me warmly, and with some magical spells on the part of Groll, I was up and about very quickly.

Soon, dressed as a Prince of the Nyarlethim should be dressed, I was wed to the radiant Princess Dweena in the great public hall with the whole Ghee as witnesses.

Great was the rejoicing in Dwornghee and laughter and tears were close akin and the wine flowed in rivers.

Married life agreed with me . . . it agreed with me very well indeed. Godranec the alien was alien no longer.

Isaac Asimov

- [ ] BEFORE THE GOLDEN AGE, Book I   22913-0   1.95
- [ ] BEFORE THE GOLDEN AGE, Book II   Q2452   1.50
- [ ] BEFORE THE GOLDEN AGE, Book III   23593-9   1.95
- [ ] THE BEST OF ISAAC ASIMOV   23653-6   1.95
- [ ] BUY JUPITER AND OTHER STORIES   23828-8   1.75
- [ ] THE CAVES OF STEEL   23782-6   1.75
- [ ] THE CURRENTS OF SPACE   23829-6   1.75
- [ ] EARTH IS ROOM ENOUGH   23383-9   1.75
- [ ] THE END OF ETERNITY   23704-4   1.75
- [ ] THE GODS THEMSELVES   23756-7   1.95
- [ ] I, ROBOT   23949-7   1.75
- [ ] THE MARTIAN WAY   23783-4   1.75
- [ ] THE NAKED SUN   23805-9   1.75
- [ ] NIGHTFALL AND OTHER STORIES   23188-7   1.75
- [ ] NINE TOMORROWS   23618-8   1.75
- [ ] PEBBLE IN THE SKY   23423-1   1.75
- [ ] THE STARS, LIKE DUST   23595-5   1.75
- [ ] WHERE DO WE GO FROM HERE?—Ed.   X2849   1.75